The Bridge from OneDayBow

The Complete Trilogy

Kathy M. Warden

Illustrations by Lyndsey Friar

With story and illustration ideas from Annette and Brad Friar

WESTBOW
PRESS®
A DIVISION OF THOMAS NELSON
& ZONDERVAN

This is a work of fiction. All of the characters, names, incidents, organizations, and dialogue in this novel are either the products of the author's imagination or are used fictitiously.

Scripture quotations are taken from the Holy Bible, New Living Translation, copyright ©1996, 2004, 2007, 2013, 2015 by Tyndale House Foundation. Used by permission of Tyndale House Publishers, Inc., Carol Stream, Illinois 60188. All rights reserved.

WestBow Press books may be ordered through booksellers or by contacting:

WestBow Press
A Division of Thomas Nelson & Zondervan
1663 Liberty Drive
Bloomington, IN 47403
www.westbowpress.com
1 (866) 928-1240

ISBN: 978-1-5127-3962-6 (sc)
ISBN: 978-1-5127-3963-3 (hc)
ISBN: 978-1-5127-3961-9 (e)

Library of Congress Control Number: 2016906675

Print information available on the last page.

WestBow Press rev. date: 09/01/2016

Dedication

Annette Friar has a firm conviction that all Christians should know and rely on the truth of God's Word—the Bible—in order to more effectively live the life He calls us to. She is equally passionate about His magnificent provision of spiritual armor, detailed in Ephesians 6, which God provides to His children. This book began because of her vision and desire, and her faith and prayers saw it through to completion. God bless you, Annette!

Acknowledgments

Brad, if there was an illustration in the dictionary for the word "servant" your face would be there! Thanks for *all* you've done and continue to do.

Lyndsey, it's been a long road, but well worth the wait! Thanks for your patient endurance, and excellence. God has gifted you greatly.

Bill, your love and encouragement have brought me much joy, and your gentle prodding has kept me going. I am blessed to have you.

Mom, you gave me life, and a legacy of love and laughter. Most important, you led me to seriously consider eternity. I will be forever grateful for you.

Pastor Nick, your faithfulness to teach the Word has inspired me and countless others to love the Truth. Thank you, and thank God for you.

And to all who faithfully prayed and carefully read—Thank you!

This book is for my Children and Grandchildren
I love each of you more than words can say—but God loves you far more!

But above all this book is dedicated to, acknowledges, and is for the King—
All honor and glory to God forever and ever! He is the eternal King, the unseen one who never dies; he alone is God. Amen. (1 Timothy 1:17 NLT)

Introduction

When Jesus walked the earth He often spoke in parables, using physical examples to illustrate spiritual truths. His parables were frequently mysterious, but concealed hidden treasure waiting to be revealed to those who cared to listen and believe. This is still true today as we read them in the pages of the Bible, in the four gospels. This is my humble attempt to imitate the Greatest Teacher in all of history. What Jesus did perfectly and with full wisdom, I can only do imperfectly, yet prayerfully and reverently, as a human disciple of the Author of our faith.

This modern-day parable has a significant twist to it: it is written in rhyme. Serious subject matter is intertwined with humor and surprise, and the rhythm of the words keeps the story flowing fluidly. It is my hope that the unique style of the story will in no way detract from its meaning, and that in all ways it will bring honor and glory to my Lord and Savior, Jesus Christ.

The characters in this book are fictional. As a way of honoring some special people in my life I have borrowed their names, but any similarity to known human beings is purely coincidental. As you read the pages of this story, you may even see yourself in some of the characters as they walk through circumstances and experiences that may be familiar to you.

There are, however, four characters who are patterned after four in the Bible. Three are recognized by Truth and Life, while the fourth is the instigator of lies and death. Most challenging to write was the dialogue of the King and His Son, because of *Who* they represent. While most of my words are not straight from the Bible, I endeavored to write carefully and respectfully. As you read this book I hope you will search the Scriptures to examine the parallels I have drawn. (Acts 17:11) My aim is that The Bridge from OneDayBow will encourage you in your faith as it points you to the Good News found in the True Word of God. (John 3:16)

Kathy Warden

Prologue

Down the road before the gate, just off the main highway,
HereAndNow looks similar to your town, you might say.
The city hums with action as people come and go.
Whether working or at play, there's no time to go slow!

On every single corner you'll see a bobble stand,
With a tempter beckoning, "Come hold them in your hand!"
And if you're smart or pretty, and have some talent too,
Bonus bobbles may pour out in triplicate to you!

The people with more bobbles are known to have more friends.
They say, "Those with the most will win where the city ends."
And tempters boast they offer fulfillment, fame, and cheer.
Such things give security—at least right now and here.

But is there more to life than just filling up a pack
With bobbles that are prone to fade, get old, chip, and crack?
Is there something better than appears in HereAndNow?
Maybe you should find out at the Bridge from OneDayBow.

Part One

The Cross Road

Do not love this world nor the things it offers you,
for when you love the world, you do not have the love
of the Father in you. For the world offers only a craving
for physical pleasure, a craving for everything we see,
and pride in our achievements and possessions.
These are not from the Father, but are from this world. And this
world is fading away, along with everything that people crave.
But anyone who does what pleases God will live forever.
(1 John 2:15-17 NLT)

Chapter 1

It seemed to take forever, but finally it's here!
They say this is the biggest and best day of the year.
The streets filled up with people two hours before the Fair,
But Tim was determined to be one of the first there.

"Excuse me, can I pass you? The contest starts at ten."
But *everyone* was trying to make it there by then.
Tim ducked beneath the field fence—which made one lady shout—
Then jumped over the rope line to take a shorter route.

He slipped around the entrance, behind the backed-up gate,
And thought, *I've got a reason—I don't have time to wait.*
After a few more detours, Tim did finally reach
The place the city mayor would open with his speech.

Tim passed by swarms of people, and lots of tempters too,
All jostling for the best seats to have the clearest view.
He sprinted up the bleachers reserved for the event,
And found a good spot facing the town's great monument.

Just outside the city's end stood the impressive site:
The tower, huge and glowing with brilliant bobble light.
Legend tells that it was built by all who lived before,
Whose lives were spent attempting to gain what they longed for.

They say the tower reaches to where they've never been,
But no one's ever passed the gate and then returned again
To HereAndNow to tell them just *what* the tower *is*.
The mayor is so proud that you'd think that it was his!

And so he tells the fable of the tower at each Fair,
And people come to listen from nearly everywhere!
As the mayor cleared his throat—right at ten till ten—
The crowd waited anxiously to hear it told again.

"The bobbles of HereAndNow make our city the best!
I'm proud to say our tower rises above the rest.
We're rolling in the bobbles and sharing in the fame,
But all of our great efforts are not *just* for the game.

"We're working for the future of all humanity.
We'll one day reach past heaven and then we'll finally be
Completely free from worry, for we will then achieve
All our minds have set to do. And that's what we believe!"

Tim's mind began to wonder, *How do they know it's true?*
Just then the mayor shouted, "This is what we'll do:
The one who is the strongest will win today's grand prize!
And I will give *one* bobble to anyone who tries."

The crowd grew excited, but Tim didn't feel the same.
"You have to be the strongest," Tim grumbled. "That's a shame.
I sure can't win this contest—and *one's* not worth the work."
A tough girl flexed her muscle and passed Tim with a smirk.

A boy pushed past him, bragging, "Hey, get out of my way!
It's obvious that *you* won't win the grand prize today."
Tim voiced his own frustration, "I won't get anywhere
Unless I get more bobbles. But I'm not sure I care."

As the crowd ran off to play, Tim slowly walked around.
Maybe he could find some bobbles lying on the ground.
Many were left there broken or with no shine at all.
Just as he was giving up he heard the tempters call.

One of them yelled out to Tim, "Come *here* to win the game!"
The tempter shined his bobbles, saying, "Boy, what's your name?"
"Some people call me Timmy, but others call me Tim."
The tempter kept polishing, trying to persuade him.

"Well, Tim, I have an offer I'm sure you can't refuse.
At the cost of your nooma, I'm here to give to you
The finest pile of bobbles that you have ever seen:
Their glow is enchanting and their quality pristine!

"You'll be the all-time winner in the Great Bobble Game.
You will be a legend in the Bobble Hall of Fame!
Hold them in your hand, boy. Have you ever seen such shine?
I'll give you all these bobbles, once your nooma is mine."

His offer was appealing, and for a little while
Tim considered gaining all the bobbles in the pile.
But something deep inside him warned him to turn and go.
A quiet voice advised him, *"Just tell the tempter, 'No!'"*

Tim didn't give his nooma to the tempters that day,
But thought about the high price they were willing to pay:
If it's all about bobbles, and bobbles bring the prize,
Why is my one nooma so important to these guys?

Chapter 2

Tim left the noisy fairgrounds and walked a tree-lined street.
A friend was also leaving, with a look of defeat.
"I'll *never* get the bobbles I need to win the game!"
His friend said, with frustration. "And I am not to blame.

"I'm not just being lazy, and I'm not dumb or weak.
I work hard to gain bobbles. I'm not some kind of freak!"
Tim knew how his friend felt because he felt that way too.
"Does anyone *really* know that the fable is true?"

But as the words were spoken, Tim wished he hadn't said
The things he had been thinking and doubting in his head.
But once he started speaking, his friend wanted to hear.
So Tim kept right on talking, though trembling with fear.

"Since no one's ever gone there and then returned to tell
If it reaches to heaven or makes the way to... Well,
They tell us to stay focused on bobbles here and now,
But have you ever heard of the Bridge from OneDayBow?"

His friend looked irritated, and said he had to go.
"Is there anyone but me who really wants to know?
I know there must be *someone!*" Tim said, impulsively,
As he stepped off the sidewalk and leaned against a tree.

Some people stopped a minute, but then quickly rushed by.
Tim wondered if they ever took time to question why
The bobbles even matter, or what they really gain.
At least from Tim's perspective, *the bobbles are a pain!*

"Have you ever seen the Bridge?" a female voice asked Tim.
He quickly turned to find out who had spoken to him.
Behind the tree, seated, was a girl he'd never met,
With nice eyes—and no bobbles! Must be new, Tim would bet.

"Hi, my name is Emma Page. I live down in the nook."
Tim thought, *She must be one of the People of the Book!*
"I've seen the Bridge and crossed it. And I have met the King."
Tim stood there and just listened, not saying anything.

"Have you ever questioned where all the bobbles come from?
Have you ever thought the game is really kind of dumb?
And what about your nooma; why do tempters want it?"
Tim felt kind of nervous but decided he should sit.

"Bobbles are important here," Tim answered cautiously.
"And I wish it wasn't so, but it's not up to me.
And why the tempters care so much, I really can't say.
My nooma must be worth a lot, judged by what they'll pay.

"Where all the bobbles come from, no one completely knows.
I've heard that tempters make them somewhere they won't disclose.
But no one really cares about the way they are made—
They only are concerned with how many they'll be paid."

Emma listened as Tim spoke about things on his mind.
Many she had spoken with were really bobble-blind.
Nothing mattered much to them except bobbles and Fairs,
But Tim had opened up like someone who really cares.

Tim went on, "To win the prize, some will do anything.
Some have even been caught at bobble counterfeiting.
I think that most are honest—at least I hope they try—
But to get a few more bobbles, they're willing to lie.

"I don't like it when they pick on people who have few.
I've often heard them saying, 'Well, what is wrong with you?
It's all because you're lazy. Why, you don't even care!
Unless you get more bobbles you won't get anywhere.'

"Everybody makes it sound so fun to play the game,
But if you're not successful, you find someone to blame."
With that, Tim grabbed his backpack and said, "I have to go."
Emma liked what he had said and quickly told him so.

"I think you're very smart, and I hope we meet again.
I'd like to take you to the Bridge since you've never been.
It's past the city's limits but not too far away.
Would you like to go there?" Tim didn't know what to say.

"Umm, let me think about it. I'll get back to you, Em."
Then Tim fled the scene, thinking, *I can't be one of them!
They say the People of the Book are all very strange.
If I crossed the Bridge, like them, I'd really have to change.*

Before Tim left she gave him a small pamphlet to read,
And told him, "In here you'll find some facts you really need.
And if you have some questions, I'd like to talk again—
Anytime or anywhere, you just tell me when."

Tim stuck it in his pocket and pushed it deep inside.
Maybe he'd read it later—someplace where he could hide.
Some folks treat you different if you think there is a King,
So for now Tim didn't need to mention anything.

Chapter 3

The Fair was in the third day, and Tim was going to try
To win a few more bobbles. So he yelled out, "Goodbye!
I'm going to the Fair, but I'll be back in a while."
His mom gave him some money—his dad just gave a smile.

His sister whined, "Can I go?" Tim left in a hurry.
Most contests are hard enough without added worry
About a little sister who would be in his way.
Their mom and dad could take her, but on some other day.

On the way he met some friends, and they were going too.
One of them was bragging loud, "I wouldn't ever do
Anything that would mess up my chance to win the game."
And then a tall girl spoke up. Tim didn't know her name.

"I'm going down this weekend with all my family
To a place where you can get a lot of bobbles—*free!*
Maybe when I get back home I'll give you one or two.
Timmy, if you'll walk with me I might give more to you."

Tim was so embarrassed, and although the girl was cute,
All his friends were laughing loud. They really had a hoot!
Tim didn't want to say it, but did it anyway:
"I don't need your free bobbles. I'll win my own today!"

He knew he hurt her feelings by the look in her eyes.
She quipped, "I only wanted to help you win a prize.
I guess you are determined to do it your own way.
I hope you can play the game as well as what you say."

And then she turned and left them, and Tim was kind of glad.
His friends kept right on laughing, trying to make him mad.
Suddenly, he didn't even care about the Fair.
When it's all said and done, he'd probably get nowhere.

Though Tim had gotten angry, it couldn't be denied
That he had lots of bobbles but wasn't satisfied.
They didn't make him happy—at least not very long.
Anyone who said they could was absolutely wrong!

So when they reached the fairgrounds, Tim went off his own way.
He wasn't in the mood now but figured he should stay.
He checked out all the contests, and even won a few,
And then looked for the tempters to see what might be new.

"Come here to trade your nooma!" Tim heard one tempter shout.
"Spend it here and rich you'll be with bobbles pouring out!"
"No, here's the place to use it!" another tempter screamed.
"Give it up and you can have more bobbles than you've dreamed!"

The tempters all seemed eager to grant their wildest dreams,
By ways that were quite simple or very far-fetched schemes.
No one should ever trust them, not what they say or do,
But people pay attention just because they want to.

Tim stopped to speak to one who acted very quirky,
Who kept on dropping bobbles because he was so jerky.
He said he had a fortune in bobble bonds and stocks,
All buried in the back field underneath purple rocks.

"Can I ask you a question?" Tim spoke sarcastically.
"Why should I even believe anything you tell me?"
The tempter gleamed with pleasure that Tim would speak to him,
And gushed, "Well, you don't have to! Just do it on a whim!

"You're better safe than sorry, is what I always say.
Try it you may like it, this could be your lucky day!
All is well that ends well when the limit is the sky!
Something's better than nothing—why, even a half-lie!"

Tim's head was almost spinning from old, worn-out clichés.
The tempter was an expert with quick, distractive phrase.
But then he added something, while motioning Tim near:
"Don't bother your mind with facts. Truth doesn't matter here."

And with that ending sentence, the tempter turned around
And picked up four cracked bobbles rolling on the ground.
He put them in a box that had words written in blue:
Return this to the tower & recycle to make new.

"What's that for?" Tim said, pointing. "You've been in the tower?"
The tempter lifted the box and quipped, "Look at the hour!
I've no more time for chatting, but I'll say this to you:
It's all about the bobbles—even if it's untrue."

"And what does *that* mean?" Tim yelled as the tempter ran off.
"I want to know the truth!" That made one tempter scoff:
"What is truth?" he chided, as he called out to the crowd.
"Make your own reality!" Then people cheered out loud.

Tim's mind was full of questions, with no one he could ask
To give him honest answers based on rock-solid facts.
He wasn't going to stay there and listen to their spiel.
Tim sighed, "I don't want more lies! I need to know what's real."

Chapter 4

That night, out in his backyard, Tim decided to look
At the pamphlet from the girl who lives down in the nook.
The title on the cover read, *The Truth Will Set You Free...*
Beneath a picture of the Bridge *...Cross here and you'll see.*

The first page asked the question: *Do you want to know*
The truth about the bobbles? Then where you need to go
Is to the Bridge, and cross it. It's there you'll plainly see
That bobbles lack real value to give security.

As Tim continued reading, beyond a doubt he knew
The words inside the booklet must be completely true:
The promise that more bobbles might win some final prize
Is absolutely fiction, all built on tempters' lies.

You spend your life focused on bobble-multiplying,
Until you get so tired you give up on trying.
It's then you might consider the tempter's offered price
For your valued nooma. Perhaps you should think twice.

The tempters are deceitful, and we all know that's true.
You only have one nooma so be careful what you do.
If you don't think it matters, you better think again:
If you give up your nooma, what happens to you then?

Tim had heard his nooma was an inner, unseen part,
Tucked snugly in his body—maybe behind his heart.
His mom had always said it's the thing that makes you, *you*.
To think you won't need it seems a foolish thing to do.

But would someone really give their nooma for the lie
Of some great hope awaiting them on the day they die?
Tim never knew a person who said that they would sell;
But if someone had done it, would they have lived to tell?

Inside, Tim felt angry at the tempters' shrewd deceit,
But also fearful dread of a probable defeat.
If there is *no* real winner in the Great Bobble Game,
Can there be a better way that's not more of the same?

But as he turned the last page, with heavy sense of need,
The words leaped into Tim's heart as he started to read:
The tempters say there's no King, or that He doesn't care;
But if you want the real Truth, perhaps you should go there.

Tim sat and thought awhile about everything he'd read.
Somehow he knew it must be right in all that it said.
Maybe he'd go to the Bridge, but couldn't act in haste—
Even though he now was sure the game is one great waste!

Chapter 5

Tim knew he had gone too long in his uncertainty.
He needed to have answers based on reality.
The bobbles hadn't filled up the emptiness within.
He grew tired of the effort and didn't try to win.

So, early in the morning, Tim headed to the nook
To try to find Emma and the People of the Book.
She was glad to see he'd come and showed him all around.
Tim noticed there was something different about the ground.

The streets all looked much cleaner—no broken bobbles there.
In fact he saw *no bobbles*, and no one seemed to care!
The place was very peaceful, which was a welcome change.
One man joked, "We're different, so some folks think we're strange."

Emma's brother told him, "Tim, this may surprise you,
But we *know* that the myth of the tower isn't true.
Despite what the tempters say, and their deceptive deeds,
We work—but not for bobbles—to meet all of our needs.

"It's great to be in the nook, but there are others who
Have been to OneDayBow and are located near you.
It's not about where you live. The King has folks spread out
In HereAndNow to show what His Kingdom is about."

Many of them told Tim of the journey that they took,
And they explained why they're called the People of the Book.
They all spoke with gratitude for what the King had done,
And together sang a song that told of the King's Son.

"There's a Bridge that we've traveled to the land of OneDayBow.
It is there we met the King, and that's why we're different now!
In His presence we've found meaning for everything we do.
We'll spend our whole life telling of the love that made us new.

"We once were separated by a deep and lengthy gorge;
No person by their strength or might could ever hope to forge.
Fear and insecurity encompassed HereAndNow,
Until the King, by His Son, made the Bridge from OneDayBow.

"We'd caused the separation by the selfish wrongs we've done,
But the King loved us so much that He gave His Only Son.
He's opened up the way for all who humbly come to see
Their need for His forgiveness and great power to set free."

Tim joined in the singing, though he didn't understand
The power of one cross on the Bridge to the King's land.
But Tim couldn't miss the fact that they lived differently.
He wanted to be like them—he wanted to be free.

Tim liked everyone there, but one stood out from the rest:
She said her name was Heidi, and told him, "I am blessed!
I have been adopted by the great and loving King.
Being His child is better than any other thing."

Tim didn't really understand what it all could mean,
But the People of the Book were the best he had seen.
None claim to be perfect, but they live like they believe
And try to share with others the things that they receive.

Tim still kept all his bobbles, though most of them he hid.
And when the tempters called out, he just ignored their bid.
Inside, something was stirring that Tim could not ignore:
There's more to life than bobbles... Something worth living for.

Chapter 6

Tim did a lot of thinking about all he had heard,
And the parts that he had read inside of the King's Word.
Some things just didn't make sense. How could he know what's true?
And when would he be certain of what he had to do?

He did believe in a King—the evidence was clear.
Still, he had some concerns and a little bit of fear.
He was firmly convinced that the tower myth is fake,
But after being tricked before feared a new mistake.

So on a warm and sunny day he set out to find
The answers to questions still rolling around his mind.
Emma promised to meet him behind the Market Place,
And as he turned the bend he was glad to see her face.

Emma's wave was friendly and her smile was quick and wide,
But Tim's inner nervousness was hard for him to hide.
His friends were pestering him about playing the game,
And spreading lots of rumors that Emma was to blame.

But Emma was a real friend—the best he ever had.
When friends spoke badly of her, it really made him mad.
"Hi Timmy," Emma called out. "I'm happy we can meet."
She pointed to a log and said, "Want to have a seat?"

The Book was there beside her—she takes it everywhere.
Tim knew his deepest questions would find the answers there.
Emma was about his age, but she knew the Book well.
She read it very often, and loved it, you could tell.

As Tim sat down beside her, he told her he was glad
For someone who would listen to the questions he had.
Not only would she listen, she'd use the Book to find
Answers that were based on Truth, not made up in her mind.

"Emma, I have been thinking," Tim's words came carefully.
"Some things are still confusing and don't make sense to me.
Why is the King so far away? Why doesn't He live here?
It seems like... if He loves us, He would want to be near.

"If we saw Him every day, more people would believe.
And He could stop the tempters and others who deceive.
It's real hard to comprehend a King that you can't see.
But I want to understand. Emma, can you help me?"

Emma opened up the Book: "In the beginning, Tim,
This big world we live in was totally made by Him."
Tim didn't understand that—it wasn't what he'd heard—
But decided to listen before he'd say a word.

"It wasn't always like this. When everything began,
The King was here along with one woman and one man.
But there was a rebellion to undermine His rule.
When the King's Word was doubted, they were easy to fool.

"Natas, a shrewd deceiver, disguised evil as good.
He said the King was lying and that the woman could
Be just as wise as the King by choosing her own way.
It caused a separation that continues today.

"It wasn't just that one time, it wasn't just that day,
It wasn't only those two who chose to disobey.
The King has authority to decide wrong and right,
But everyone wants to do what's best in their own sight."

Tim understood what she meant. He always knew inside
That there is a right and wrong, and it couldn't be denied.
Still, it seems perplexing that a King so great would be
Allowing strong-willed people to live defiantly.

Before Tim voiced his question, Emma said, "See this page:
'Why do people plot in vain? Why do the nations rage?'
Many stand against the King, and oppose His Son.
He could have judged quickly, but do you know what He's done?

"The King sent His Son for us—*a Bridge had to be made*.
We can only choose to go because of what *He* paid.
He's willing to forgive wrongs, and save us from our fear
Of what happens when we die." She wiped away a tear.

Surprised by Emma's passion, and struck by words she said,
Uneasily, Tim asked her, "What happens when we're dead?
I know the heart stops pumping blood when your life is through…
I guess I'm asking about the nooma inside you."

Tim had asked the question that people don't like to raise.
No one wants to think about the ending of their days.
But Tim had always wondered, and now needed to know.
Emma answered, softly, "So, you wonder where you'll go?

"When you meet the King by faith, your nooma is made new.
You will safely live with Him when this first life is through.
For those who will not trust the King before their final day,
Their forfeited nooma exists… in a sorry way.

"Once you pass the city's end the time is then too late
To receive the King's Nooma. No one should hesitate!
The choice is yours to make, Tim. It says so in His Word.
I'm praying you respond soon to the Truth you have heard."

She put the Book in his hands and said, "Look at this part.
The King says we need to trust Him with all of our heart.
And He will help you do it—it's not all up to you.
Talk to Him about it and you'll see what He can do."

Tim read the Book a minute, then closed it with a smile.
Emma passed a note, then said, "Here, read this in a while."
She put the Book in her pack, saying, "See you soon, Tim."
He answered, "Thank you Emma." Then she quickly hugged him.

On the way home, Tim thought about what it means to pray.
Talking to an unseen King? What should he even say?
Would the King listen to him? Tim decided to try:
"Hello King, my name is Tim..." Then he let out a sigh.

"I don't know what I should say. The words are hard to find...
Maybe You already know the thoughts inside my mind.
Some people say You aren't real, but I believe You are.
The place You're in—OneDayBow—King, is that very far?

"Emma tells me You're perfect in all You say and do,
And it's only by Your Son that I can come to You.
I've done a lot of wrong things. But worst of all I try
To pretend You don't exist. Guess I believed the lie.

"I can't go to the Bridge now—it's not what I had planned.
My mom and dad don't know You, and they won't understand.
I want to go there one day. I'd really like to see...
If I do come to the Bridge... King, will You welcome me?"

Tim had reached his driveway, but before he climbed the hill
He said, "King, just one more thing... Please help me want Your will."
Somehow Tim knew for certain the King had heard his prayer,
And he'd never doubt again the King is really there.

Chapter 7

Tim stared up at the ceiling, then turned from side to side.
His mind wouldn't take a rest, no matter what he tried.
He did all he could think of to help him fall asleep,
But gave up when he counted out seven hundred sheep.

He kicked the covers off him and climbed out of his bed.
A million fleeting thoughts kept on running through his head:
What's it like to cross the Bridge? What happens if I won't?
Will I be glad I went there, or sorry if I don't?

Tim looked outside his window and glimpsed the monument.
He thought about those now gone and wondered where they went.
Were they up in the tower trying to reach the sky?
Or was their nooma made new before their time to die?

Tim thought about his Grandpa, who'd gone out of his way
To show how much he loved him. Grandpa would often say,
"You only have one nooma, so think before you choose.
Meet the King at OneDayBow to gain what you can't lose."

His mind became more settled as he recalled each word.
As a little boy it was the best news that he heard.
Somehow through his growing he had left those words behind,
But tonight he found they were still written on his mind.

Tim smiled as he remembered the lady down the street
Had told him of the loving King that he could one day meet.
And there were many others who told him it was true:
They'd crossed the Bridge, met the King, and gained a Nooma *new*.

But deep inside Tim wondered, *Will I be good enough?*
I've done a lot of bad things and some really dumb stuff.
Suddenly, Tim realized that more than anything
He needed forgiveness and acceptance from the King.

Beside his bed he noticed a partly folded note.
That's right, it came from Emma! She'd written a Book quote:
"All who come to Me in faith, I will not send away."
The King's Son made that promise! Tim decided to pray.

"I've heard You are right and good, and never would deceive.
So I have every reason to trust You and believe
Who You are, and what You say, as real authority.
I believe *You are the Truth*—that's my security."

Finally he fell asleep sometime before midnight,
With a sense of deep peace that he would be alright.
Since the King's Son built the Bridge—and paid the full cost too—
Tim didn't need to be afraid, but knew what he must do.

Chapter 8

As the sun was coming up, Tim jumped out of his bed
With thoughts and plans from last night still firmly in his head.
At last he was certain that there was no other way.
He would not turn back from his course—this would be the day.

He grabbed his pack of bobbles, in case there was a cost,
And if it took all he had he wouldn't count it lost.
It was a big decision that was not lightly made,
But Tim was sure it would be worth any price he paid.

Tim passed the mocking tempters and set out for the ridge.
"We won't want your nooma if you choose to cross that Bridge."
"You lose your hope of bobbles if you choose to leave here!"
The tempters' threats intended to make Tim turn in fear.

But Tim would not be bullied—the Bridge was in his sight.
His bobble-toting friend jeered: "Hey, Tim, you're not too bright.
Why would you waste your nooma on something you can't see?
Don't risk all your bobbles for a King that may not be!"

"And if there is a King, He's an ogre in disguise!
He claims that He is *the Truth,* and we're all lost in lies.
But if He's such a good King, why doesn't He come here
And bring us lots of bobbles?" one girl said with a sneer.

They kept up all their taunting, but now were far behind:
"Why would Timmy make this choice? He must have lost his mind!"
"You're gonna be sorry if you go to OneDayBow.
There ain't nothin' better than livin' in HereAndNow."

Tim paused there for a moment while standing on the ridge.
He'd heard some hadn't come back after they crossed the Bridge.
But something drew him onward—*Someone* he couldn't see—
And so he kept on going, advancing eagerly.

Tim could think more clearly as he left the noisy blare.
He knew that this decision was one he couldn't share.
(The choice to meet the King is a choice you make alone,
But only by that first choice the King made on His own.)

The mid-day sun shined brightly, and Tim enjoyed a breeze.
Soaring birds sang loudly as they raced between the trees.
The flow of the river was like music to his ear,
Playing out the constant tune, *"Aren't you glad that you're here?"*

This place was so much different than noisy HereAndNow.
A small sign simply marked it: *The Bridge from OneDayBow.*
No tempters were there shouting how much he could be paid,
Just someone standing—welcoming—at the Bridge He made.

"To everyone who's seeking, I'm glad you've come today.
I chose to build this Bridge so that you *can* choose My Way.
Only by this one Bridge can you enter OneDayBow.
Only by the mighty King can you have real life now."

Tim stood there for a minute and wondered, *Should I go?*
I've already come this far and now I really know.
But it's not just a side trip—the commitment's for life!
As Tim weighed out his options, the air seemed filled with strife.

He realized the cross road would change everything,
Because it must mean something to call somebody *King.*
Tim thought, *I know the Book says that if I seek I'll find...*
This choice must be determined in action, will, and mind.

The bobbles that he carried weighed heavy in his pack.
He wondered, *If I leave them here, will I want them back?*
The Man was standing, waiting—He would let Tim decide.
Tim dropped his pack completely and walked to the Man's side!

He felt his burden lighten when the bobbles went down:
Eager to leave the pressure to achieve self-renown.
But with nothing to offer, would the Man let him through?
With open arms, He told Tim, "Have I got a gift for you!

"There is no cost to cross here. I paid for everything.
I built the Bridge you couldn't to bring you to the King.
Forgiveness and acceptance are waiting there for you
From the King—My Father. He will make your nooma *new.*"

Tim quickly thanked the Son and then left his bobbles there.
He knew someone might take them, but didn't even care.
As he looked ahead and up, his future path was bright.
And as he stepped on the Bridge, he knew his choice was right.

(Standing high above the gorge—but not out of thin air—
The Bridge spans a vast distance to get from here to there.
And all who choose the cross road, relying on the Son,
Find the Bridge is sure and strong because of all He's done.)

Tim set out on its curved path, and suddenly he found
He was no longer upright but had turned upside down!
It scared him for a moment, but when the moment passed
He knew *he* was right side up and so began to laugh.

Excitement getting stronger, Tim eagerly rushed on.
His nooma grew warmer as he glimpsed the scene beyond:
A place of peace and beauty where everything is new,
And even pavement sparkles more than the bobbles do!

Suddenly, Tim saw the One who outshines everything!
Nothing had prepared him for the greatness of the King.
As Tim stepped into His light, he easily saw how
Everyone and everything will humbly one day bow.

Awestruck, Tim stood silently—amazed to be so near.
But the King's words gave comfort that pushed away all fear:
"You're able to approach Me in spite of wrong you've done,
For I so loved the world that I gave My Only Son."

Tim tried to say the Son should not have to pay the cost,
But knew without His sacrifice all hope would be lost.
Tim kneeled and said, "I've done wrong…" The King said, "I forgive."
Tim whispered, *"I believe You."* He answered, "Now, you live!"

It seemed that very moment that everything was changed.
Had the brain cells in his head somehow been rearranged?
The tempters' lies and schemes were exposed by what is true:
The King's Son gives new life when His Nooma lives in you!

And then it made sense to Tim, why tempters often pled
To take a person's nooma—they want to see them dead!
Not just the end Tim once feared, but ending anything
That might lead them to the Son and new life in the King.

Now that Tim had crossed the Bridge and met the King at last,
He recognized dishonesty had held him in the past:
The legends of the city, and bobble-quest from youth,
Are sinister deceptions to distract from the Truth!

But he also knew the King had People in that place
To tell the Truth, resist lies, and speak about His grace.
Because they cared enough to tell Tim about the way,
He met the Son and took His cross to the King that day!

Tim thought of the people still deceived in HereAndNow,
Too busy chasing bobbles to consider OneDayBow.
They don't think they need the King, but that is such a lie!
Tim thought, *I have to tell them... at least, I need to try.*

But who'd want to leave the King to go back to that town,
To try to convince them their thinking is upside down?
This Kingdom is Tim's real home, and it will always be;
But if no one will tell them, how will they be set free?

Tim's words remained unspoken, yet he knew the King heard
Everything his mind had thought before he said a word.
Then apprehension ended at the words of the Son:
"The journey doesn't end here—in fact, it's just begun!"

Part Two

Stand!

Therefore, put on every piece of God's armor so you will be able to resist the enemy in the time of evil. Then after the battle you will still be standing firm. (Ephesians 6:13 NLT)

Chapter 9

"This place is so amazing!" Tim said excitedly.
"I'm really here—and *it's real!* I wish my friends could see!"
He'd left behind his bobbles but had gained so much more.
OneDayBow was better than all that he'd hoped for.

Tim thought about the others living in HereAndNow,
So occupied with bobbles that they could not see how
The Bridge, the King, and His Kingdom could really be true.
But Tim could clearly see what exists beyond their view.

Until Tim had crossed over, he too was just as blind:
Bobble-quest certainly shaped and influenced his mind.
But now he knew the Truth has great power to set free.
Tim shouted past the mountains, "Cross over and you'll see!

"HereAndNow is upside down—it's not what you believe.
The tempters lure with bobbles to mislead and deceive.
The King wants every person to come and meet His Son;
Cross the Bridge *to* OneDayBow and find out what He's done."

Tim couldn't wait to tell them, and yet dreaded the day
He might have to leave the King. He'd really rather stay.
Though torn between the two things, he knew the King would lead
In the way He knows is best, so others can be freed.

The King knew Tim's deepest thoughts and spoke with mystery:
"Even while in HereAndNow, you still will be with Me.
I am the eternal King, not limited by place.
My Kingdom is not bound by confines of time and space."

Tim couldn't really fathom how His Kingdom could be
Unconfined by time and space, but observed presently.
Tim's mind played with the riddle till he heard the King say
Something about tempters, then, "Your training starts today.

"Because of all you're facing, your journey will be slow.
But throughout the adventure you'll learn things you must know.
So keep this in your mind in whatever you go through:
You won't do this on your own—*My Nooma goes with you.*

"He will guide into all Truth as you walk in His way,
Teaching and reminding you of My Word, day by day.
I've put My Word in writing. I'm giving you My Book
So you can learn from Me. Just open it and look."

Tim had seen the Book before—at least one just like it.
He'd read through part of Emma's. She told him that it lit
Her steps and pathway in the Kingdom of OneDayBow.
Tim didn't see a light attached, and asked, "This works, how?"

The King said, "Navigation is surer by fixed light:
My Book provides vision more reliable than sight.
Who I am and what I speak is in here to be heard,
And it is by My Nooma you understand My Word.

"So when you're confused or scared, or if you start to doubt,
My Book will point you to Me and help you figure out
What is *really* going on beyond what you can see.
Be aware of the battle, and act accordingly."

The King handed Tim a belt, and said, "You need to wear
This Truth belt tightly on you. Tim, always keep it there.
You need this firm reminder: *by My Truth take your stand.*
This piece is invaluable on the path that is planned."

The belt fit on Tim loosely—his pants hung kind of low.
The Son told him, "Cinch it up. In time you're gonna grow.
Truth is always the best choice, whatever life may bring.
When you choose to live that way you're honoring the King."

Now filled with great excitement, Tim set his foot to go
Off in a direction that he didn't even know.
But the Son knew the path and His Book provided light.
The belt kept Tim centered as Truth held him upright.

The view was so breathtaking—the mountains majesty!
It was like he'd been born blind but now at last could see.
Some things Tim barely noticed before in HereAndNow,
Looked clearer and much brighter to him in OneDayBow.

The sun began its setting and color filled the sky,
As orange and red reflected on birds that sailed up high.
And as the twilight faded, stars lit up all around.
Tim smiled with satisfaction and stretched out on the ground.

Gazing into the night sky, Tim suddenly felt small
As he observed the vastness and beauty of it all.
That portion of the sky was a glimpse of so much more.
Tim marveled at the bright stars: *Who do they sparkle for?*

It seemed like a strange question, but Tim was always taught
It all exists by accident. But it's not what they thought.
The King is the Creator—it all was made by Him!
And somehow in that moment it all made sense to Tim.

He made the stars above me, and holds them up in space.
Because of His great power they all stay in their place.
None of this is here by chance—it had to be designed:
Creation is magnificent, chance is dumb and blind.

Tim opened up the King's Book and read, "Let there be light!"
He spoke it in to being, then divided day from night.
He separated waters, made sun and stars and more.
He created all these things—and that was by day four!

Next He made sea creatures and birds that soar the skies.
On day six came animals, and then a great surprise:
He made man in His image, and made a woman too.
All He made was very good! Creation's work was through.

Tim was thoroughly amazed by all he read and saw.
What a great Designer—He made gravity a law!
He sustains the universe, holding it together;
He is King of everything, now and forever!

Excited and exhausted, Tim closed the Book to sleep.
He had a lot of questions but knew that they would keep.
Now his life had purpose like he never had before,
Knowing his Creator is a King worth living for.

Chapter 10

Wide-eyed at the daybreak and eager to see more,
Tim beamed with expectation of what was next in store.
Overwhelmed with gratitude for all that he had gained,
His thankfulness flowed over like a flood uncontained.

Tim paused there on the mountain to meet with the King's Son,
Saying, "I'm very grateful for all the King has done.
How can I repay You? What can I do for You
To show that I am thankful for making my life new?"

"Tim, I don't expect you to pay back anything.
You received this freely when you trusted in the King.
But if you're really asking, 'What does the King require?'
Trust and obey Him always, in actions and desire.

"Although that may sound easy it's very hard to do,
But you have resources now that can enable you.
Our Nooma that We gave you, He isn't just a *thing*;
He is the living Presence and power of the King.

"Yield quickly to His leading—in His strength take your stand—
Even through the hardest times of rigorous demand.
He's with you on your journey, and He will help you pray."
And with those words the Son sent Tim off in the right way.

Before he traveled too far, Tim saw a great surprise:
People of all ages, every color, shape, and size
Were gathered there, united, as children of the King.
Together, as one family, they all joined in to sing.

"Thank You King for bringing us to You in OneDayBow.
Please make us good examples to those in HereAndNow.
Because of You, we are new, and now we clearly see
How far from Truth we once were—but You have set us free.

"Blinded by the bobble's shine and gripped by their strong pride;
Your love becomes devalued when Your Truth is despised.
HereAndNow is upside down because wrong is called right.
But when we choose to cross Your Bridge, You restore our sight."

As he watched and listened to every girl and boy,
Tim had never heard such singing filled with so much joy.
They danced, sang, and did cartwheels—pure laughter filled the air—
Without a single bobble, without a single care!

"Hi, my name is Brianna, and he's my brother Bryce.
We noticed that you're new here and thought it would be nice
To join you on your journey. We've been here for a while,
But there's always more to learn!" the girl said with a smile.

So the three walked together while Bryce filled Timmy in,
Often reading in the Book that the King had given.
"It's all in here to help you with the answers you'll need.
No matter what might happen, you must let the Truth lead.

"Your journey will be rugged—there's danger in the land.
Sometimes you'll want to hide, but you must choose to stand
In the power of the King and by His promised might.
His Nooma is inside you urging you to choose right."

Brianna warned, "Be ready for tempters up ahead.
They want you to doubt the King and choose their way instead.
Remember they are tricky and will try to deceive,
So know what's in the Book and then live like you believe."

And with those words they parted at the end of the day,
Certain they would meet again somewhere along the way.
But as they left, Tim questioned, "Tempters are here with me?
I thought that once I crossed the Bridge I was *then* set free."

Tim wondered for a moment about the tempting foe,
But figured, if the time comes, the Book would help him know.
And so he stopped and read it until he had to sleep,
Yawning, "That's enough for now. I'm sure the rest will keep."

Chapter 11

Tim woke up feeling rested. There was so much to see,
He couldn't wait to start the day back on his journey.
He marveled at the landscape and gazed at all the sights.
Not wanting to miss a thing, he could've walked for nights!

But as he turned the corner, down at the river bend,
A man was standing, waiting—he said he was a friend.
Though Tim felt apprehensive, he just wanted to know:
Is this man a real King's friend, or is he the King's foe?

The man reached in his satchel and lifted something out.
With a toothy-grin, he said, "Now, that's what life's about!"
As Tim moved in much closer, the man's fingers unfurled:
Holding one HUGE bobble, he asked, "Want to have the world?"

Tim backed up in a hurry and said, "You *are* a foe!
They warned me I would meet you, and I want you to know
I am now the King's child and completely bobble-free.
And you can't have the Nooma that's here inside of me!"

The man said, "Don't be hasty and run amuck with doubt.
I've got the best intentions. I'm here to help you out!
You must know that I'm mentioned inside of *that* King's Book.
If you don't believe me you can open it and look.

"But if you're going back *there*, you'll need at least a few.
Unless you have *some* bobbles, they won't listen to you.
They never will believe you. They'll think you're a weird one.
Without a single bobble, they won't care what you've done."

Tim listened to the sales pitch—which made a lot of sense.
And *if* he came from the King, Tim could drop his defense.
But when he eyed the bobbles, he noticed the belt slipped.
And as he filled his pockets, the belt dropped and he tripped!

Suddenly, the man turned mean: "I see just how you are.
You're any easy one to trick, and sure won't get too far.
You say you are *that* King's child, and that you're bobble-free,
But when I made the offer you were quick to agree!

"Don't tell me you're *that* King's child, after what you just did!
You're not any different from every other kid.
You still do want the bobbles, and that you can't deny.
You can't convince me of it, so don't bother to try."

The tempter poked at Tim's chest, filling his mind with fright.
Although the foe had tricked him, Tim feared his words were right.
As pocketfuls of bobbles spilled out onto the ground,
Tim searched himself for courage, but none was to be found.

Then suddenly, Tim recalled something the King had said:
"I will be with you always," kept running through Tim's head.
He bent and pulled the belt up and cinched it tight in place.
As he loudly yelled out, "Help!" fear covered the foe's face!

The tempter quickly backed up, then pivoted and ran,
Just as the Son's voice boomed out: "Don't come back here again!
Be warned! He belongs to me, and in My might he'll stand.
No one can snatch him from Me, or from My Father's hand."

Running to where the Son stood—the very safest place!—
Tim knew that he had let Him down and felt such disgrace.
Humbly, Tim said, "I'm sorry." He then went on to say,
"I know I messed up badly and failed the King today.

"I let the belt of Truth slip when I believed that fake.
I didn't need those bobbles. I made a big mistake.
I hope You can forgive me and help me try again.
I promise to do better than what I did just then."

The Son said, "I forgive you. But you must realize
That to stand against tempters means rejecting their lies.
Don't believe it when they say what's written in My Book.
The Truth you need is found when you open it and look.

"Look Tim, right here it's written, '*The Truth will set you free*.'
When he offered bobbles, did you think he spoke for Me?
The tempters are deceivers who distort what is right.
When you know and live Truth, that's when they lose the fight.

"You need some more equipping—it's Mine—for you to wear.
I'll fasten it securely so it's sure to stay there.
My righteousness now covers you completely, not in part.
And it's no coincidence this fits over your heart."

The Son said, "It's effective against accusing foe
Who point out all your wrongness—and love to tell you so.
But through success and failure, this lesson must be learned:
I've made you right with the King, and that cannot be earned."

Tim eyed his new apparel. He liked the way it shined.
A tempter couldn't miss it, unless totally blind!
The Son said, "Tim, be certain that real security
Cannot come from anything but being right with Me.

"Continue on your journey—it's no time to turn back.
I've given you provision so no good thing you'll lack.
The lessons that you've learned here must not be left behind.
Hold firmly to My Truth and let it renew your mind."

Tim started to feel stronger and well prepared to go.
"He will not trick me next time—I'll tell that tempter so!"
And as the Son heard Tim speak, His words came with a smile:
"This one has a lot to learn. It's gonna take a while."

Chapter 12

Tim's trip was going smoothly—at least for the past day—
And self-assurance led as he turned off the straightway.
A sign read, *Here's the shortcut that leads to HereAndNow.*
Caution, this way's not open to those from OneDayBow!

Tim pondered for a moment, "Hmm, should I go this way?
If I were to ask the King, I wonder what He'd say."
Before he asked the question, his mind already made
The wrong choice—yes, the shortcut! (But shouldn't Tim have prayed?!)

It only took a minute to regret what he chose:
All at once Tim sank in mud, almost up to his nose!
He couldn't even cry out for help to be set free.
And as he tried to pull out, a tempter laughed with glee!

This tempter looked much different, yet strangely much the same.
He bent down next to Tim, saying, "Natas is my name.
How dare you try to cross here! You must have read the sign.
That King must have told you that HereAndNow is *now* mine!"

Tim could barely breathe from fright—never mind the mud!
And each beat of his heart raced a faster, deeper thud.
The Book, and Emma, warned him of this shrewd enemy,
But Tim was caught off guard by his harsh reality.

45

Natas laughed and boldly said, "Most think that I'm not real.
It's easy to deceive those who trust in what they *feel*.
If they don't know they're captives, they won't try to be free.
And my gates firmly hold those who blindly follow me.

"I give them lots of bobbles to keep them occupied.
I cannot let you tell them that I have always lied!
They're *willingly* deceived by the bobbles' blinding glow.
It's all about the bobbles! That's all they need to know."

Tim was filled with much more fright than he had ever been.
Will the Son come save me soon? If so, please tell me when!
He didn't have enough strength to ask for help or shout,
But His Nooma intervened and Tim's request went out.

It seemed to take forever, but that's just how it seemed,
Till Natas glanced past Tim's face, looked terrified, and screamed!
"So *You've* come here to help him! He walked into this place..."
Though Natas spoke quite bravely, fear covered his whole face.

"Just take him, and good riddance! I don't want him around!
But we will meet again, Tim, perhaps in your own town."
The Son took hold of Tim's hand and pulled him from the pit.
Tim slowly stopped his shaking and exclaimed, "This is it!

"This journey is too hard, and I've fallen once again.
You said You wouldn't leave me and told me I'm Your friend.
So how could You just let me wander into this trap?
The least You could have done is supply me with a map!

"And is it really true that Natas owns HereAndNow?
He's blinded them with bobbles—they can't see OneDayBow!
I only took a shortcut... Okay, I went too fast.
And now I've gone and ruined it. How long will this trip last?!"

The Son said, "Tim, you must know there's only one right way:
You must rely on My Word and then choose to obey.
Though you now belong to Me, you have to realize
That till you're made perfect you're susceptible to lies.

"Before you ever came here, Tim—long before your birth—
There were just two people living on the earth.
The King supplied all their needs to make their lives complete,
But gave one firm restriction, which should have stopped deceit.

"Natas, the deceiver, approached with a bold lie:
'If you deny the King's Word, you will not *surely* die.
Your eyes will be opened, and you will be discerning.'
They chose to disobey through disbelief of the King.

"After that—as the King warned—death was a sad, hard fact.
Natas had a foothold then, as people knew they lacked
The means to rise above the end that filled their minds with fear.
And life became all about 'living for now and here.'

"It wasn't just that one time, it wasn't just that day,
It wasn't just those first two who chose to disobey.
Deceived by self and Natas, the things people desired
Turned them from the King's Truth and the faith He required."

"Why would they believe Natas?" Tim spoke emphatically.
"It's clear that he's a liar! Why can't the people see?"
But as Tim raised the question, he knew he'd fallen too.
With a humble voice, he asked, "So, what did the King do?"

"In many ways He reached out," the Son said quietly,
"To warn of the great danger of living carelessly.
Many doubted his judgment, while others tried to hide.
It caused a separation as deep as it is wide."

"And so I came to the world on behalf of the King,
To tell them of His great love, and repeat His warning:
'It matters how you live—I'm aware of what you do.
Trust and obey My Word so it may go well with you.'

"Many didn't believe Me, or the message We said.
Some thought they'd be better off if only I was dead.
I took on the punishment because I came to save,
Defeating Natas' death-grip when I conquered the grave."

Tim listened intently to all that the King's Son said.
Some of it he remembered from the King's Word he'd read.
The Son then asked, "Do you know the cause of what I've done?
The King so loved the world that He gave His only Son.

"Those gates Natas erected cannot stand securely,
When those who are still living take My cross to be free.
All who come to Me in faith, their eyes I will unveil.
Natas can't block My Kingdom: his gates shall not prevail!"

In awe, Tim said, "So that's how You got scars on Your hands—
Bridging the great divide that spans between the two lands.
Since it came *from* OneDayBow, and was built by You alone,
No one can take credit that they get here on their own."

"Well said, Tim," the Son replied. "And others need to know
There are not *many ways*, but just *one way* to go:
No one comes to My Father except by Me, His Son.
We're perfectly united—I and the Father are One."

"I don't understand it all," Tim said, "but this is clear:
If not for the Bridge You made, I couldn't have come here.
There is no other way but the one the King provides,
Through You, by Your sacrifice, and nothing else besides."

The Son smiled at Tim and said, "I'm glad you crossed the Bridge.
The next part of the path takes you up along this ridge.
If you don't walk carefully you'll stumble passing through,
So here are some peace shoes that are fitted just for you."

Tim slipped on the shoes and said, "Now that's a funny name!
Why would You call them pea shoes?" Tim laughingly exclaimed.
The Son joined in the laughter, "Not pea shoes, Tim—no, *peace*.
They're called peace shoes because you go to offer release."

"These shoes are pretty heavy." Tim walked toward the Son.
The Son replied, "They're sturdy for the journey you're on.
They'll help you to go further, and sometimes just to stand.
Most of all you'll need their grip in that upside-down land.

"You have good news to take them of the King's promised peace.
Those who choose to cross My Bridge, Natas has to release.
Keep these shoes on—be ready!—and walk purposefully.
Be aware of the pitfalls and don't act carelessly."

Now armed with the equipment the Son had provided,
Tim set out on the pathway, prepared and excited:
Breastplate of righteousness on; peace shoes upon his feet;
The belt of Truth in place, and the Book to fight deceit.

Chapter 13

Tim's next path spanned the meadow, where tempters seldom go.
(But in that place of leisure, self-trust will often grow.)
Each time he shunned the tempters, Tim's courage seemed to soar.
Somehow he thought he couldn't be tempted anymore.

While he walked he thought about how very far he'd come,
From tempters treating him like he was completely dumb!
Then, down beside the water, Tim saw them sitting there:
Three tempters making small-talk while seated in their chair.

Tim paused there for a moment—he thought he heard his name!
"Tim has gotten very good at putting us to shame.
He's not an easy target. He really is quite shrewd.
I must say, I am impressed with his brave attitude."

Tim stood there very silent—a smile covered his face—
As he heard one tempter say, "Tim's put us to disgrace!
Let's find another victim that's easier to fool.
I'm afraid he's beaten us." Then they jumped in the pool.

So, feeling quite elated, Tim forged on straight ahead
With all their compliments now resounding in his head.
He thought he might go back there and chase them from that place.
He'd make them regret the day they dared to show their face!

As Tim walked on the belt slipped, and so he took it off.
He loosened up the breastplate; he thought it made him cough.
The Book was dropped; his arms tired of packing it around.
The shoes came off so he could walk barefoot on the ground.

Tim said aloud, "No tempter should cross my path today.
If one starts to hassle me, I know just what I'll say:
'Listen to your buddies and keep your distance from me.'
If they want to mess with Tim, trouble they're gonna see."

Almost before he finished, Tim's words abruptly stopped.
Straight ahead he saw a sight that made his jawbone drop:
The three who had been swimming were waiting for him there.
One remarked, "Well, here you are. You've walked into our lair!

"You thought that you were so tough. You thought you could not fall.
But look, you've been tripped-up by the oldest trick of all!"
Another tempter chided, as Tim began to slide,
"It seems you've slid into the slippery muck of pride.

"Where is all your equipment? You thought *you* were that strong?
You didn't know our plan was to catch you all along?
It really wasn't too hard—look at your swollen head.
It's clear to see you ate up each tempting word we said.

"Didn't *that* Book tell you, 'Pride comes before a fall'?
Now you're covered with the muck and much too proud to call
Out to *that* Son to save you. Now really, why should He?
You got yourself in this mess, so now get yourself free."

Tim struggled for a moment to try and crawl away,
Sighing loud, "This takes the cake as my very worst day!
Not only was I set up, I chose to take the bait
Of trusting in *my* greatness—which turned out not so great."

Tim groaned, "I got myself here and must get myself out."
But deep inside he heard the words, *"Why not just cry out?*
If you trust in your own strength, your pride will only grow.
Humbly call on the Son, NOW! Tim, act on what you know!"

Tim was so embarrassed that he'd done it once again,
But in the muck he felt this was the lowest he had been.
The tempters stood there gloating, and one said gleefully,
"You're too proud to call for help—you'll have to stay with me!"

Suddenly, he realized the charge of pride was true.
Tim thought too much of himself, but now he clearly knew
That what he thought was his strength was weakness in disguise.
(Pride does not produce courage, but feeds on tempters' lies.)

"Help!" The word came, pleading. Tim yelled out louder then:
"King's Son, please come and save me! I've fallen once again.
I know it was my own fault—I willingly admit—
But trust You will forgive me because You promised it.

"Your Book tells me that Your strength is perfect when I'm weak,
And that You will be found by the person who will seek.
I'm weak—I cannot hide it—and I am seeking You.
I'm helpless in my own strength. Please come to my rescue!"

Tim started to feel stronger but knew that it must be
Not by *his* might or power that he was breaking free.
Just then the tempters scattered at the sight of the Son
Coming to Tim's aid, again, in spite of what he'd done.

Shivering cold, Tim shuddered, "… a stupid thing I did.
I'd have been much better off if I had only hid!
I brought it on my own self… and yet You came to save.
My vain imagination convinced me I was brave."

The Son smiled. "Now you see the deceitfulness of pride:
It made you think you were strong, but instead made you slide
Into the murky mire that seemed to weigh a ton.
True strength was only shown when you called out for the Son."

Tim offered no excuses but chose humility.
"I can't blame the tempters for the fault inside of me.
The pride rose up so easy, it had to be put down.
The muck certainly did that—it slid me to the ground!

"Though I do admit my wrong, I still don't understand
How come all these tempters are permitted in Your land.
Why do they come to tempt me? What purpose can they serve?
Seems to me, their presence here is perfectly absurd.

"You say that there is peace here, and yes, I do have peace—
But I would be more peaceful if their visits would cease.
You say that I am free now, and yes, I know I'm free—
But I'd feel much freer if they weren't harassing me."

The Son smiled for a moment, and then He stood there still.
"You've asked honest questions that regard My Father's will.
If the King is ruling over all that you can see,
It must seem strange in His land that tempters *seem* quite free.

"But the way that it may seem is not the way it is.
The King decides what He permits: the final word is His.
Despite what the tempters try they can't thwart what I've done.
Their schemes turn against them when you choose to trust the Son.

"You'll find it's often easy to go off your own way,
Forgetting that you need Me through each and every day.
If your path is simple and completely trouble-free,
How long will it take till you try to walk without Me?"

Tim didn't give an answer to what the King's Son said,
But tried to solve that conflict inside of his own head:
Temptations all around me prove that I'm prone to fall.
Is the purpose so I'll trust the King's Son above all?

The Son said to Tim, firmly, "I have equipped you to
Stand against the tempter's schemes that want to defeat you.
But you can only stand fast because of what I've done.
And if you trust in *your* strength, the conflict won't be won.

"Remember the tempters know you have Our Nooma now—
That was sealed the day you met the King in OneDayBow.
They can't separate you from the love you have in Me.
And one day, in My Final Place, you'll be tempter-free."

Tim gathered the equipment that he had laid aside,
When he forgot the battle and trusted his own pride.
And then the Son said, "Here Tim, this helmet's for your head.
I think the swellings down from the flattery they said."

Embarrassed, Tim asked the Son, "What will this helmet do?"
The Son replied, "This will protect, and will remind you
That it's not by your own strength that you walk in this place.
There is no room for boasting—I keep you by My grace.

"I've rescued you from far more than you can comprehend.
I've given you a new life and count you as My friend.
This helmet of salvation deflects the tempters' lie
That says you cannot be saved—and other tricks they'll try."

With the helmet on his head, Tim said, "I guess I'll be
Facing more tempter's schemes. But now I kinda see
That there is some benefit in every painful test:
I'm reminded I need You, and that Your way is best."

In days ahead when Tim faced the tempter's shrewd deceit,
With all their accusations and threats of his defeat;
Tim learned *both* doubt and pride will make pitfalls for his way.
The helmet of salvation is needed every day.

Chapter 14

Tim was filled with gratitude and endeavored to show
Real commitment to the King. He wanted Him to know
That he'd follow the Son's steps and do what was required
To live his life to please Him. That is what Tim desired.

One day the Son said to Tim, "I have a job for you."
Tim answered, "I am ready, just tell me what to do.
Whatever You are needing, whatever You require,
I'll do my best to give to You whatever You desire.

"Just tell me what You're wanting, and I will meet Your needs."
The Son answered him softly, "It's time to pull some weeds."
"Pull weeds?" was all Tim could say. Had he heard the Son right?
He'd gladly serve Him bravely and walk through darkest night!

Certainly, he was worthy of more than pulling weeds.
The Son saw Tim's face, and spoke, "You said you'd meet My needs.
Well, that is what I need, Tim. And it is what you need.
It's time to learn the difference between good plant and weed."

Without any real fervor, Tim decided to be
The very best weed-picker the Son would ever see!
But after just one hour, Tim asked, "Is this job done?"
"Be steadfast in your work, Tim," answered the watching Son.

And so Tim pushed on further, though lacking in true zeal.
"It's important what you do—don't go by how you feel.
Emotions are deceptive and can't make you obey.
You must *choose* to obey Me." That's all the Son would say.

He stepped back from the weed patch, and out of Tim's clear view.
Without the Son's watching-eye, would Tim still see this through?
Would he faithfully obey and do what the Son asks?
Would he think it important to finish up His tasks?

Tim thought about the Son's words, and thought about the King.
Shouldn't he give his best to what the Son was asking?
Although he didn't like it, he would choose to obey.
And if he had to do this, he'd do it all the way!

Tim thought the work was finished long before the sun set,
But the Son stepped in and said, "You're not quite finished yet.
The weeds that you have pulled up can't be left lying there,
Or all the seeds will scatter and blow into the air.

"The reason to pull weeds is so they won't multiply.
After they are rooted up, in the fire they must die.
If they're not fully dealt with, there'll be more than you know.
And when the weeds take over, good seed is hard to grow."

By the time that he finished it was cold, dark, and late.
Tim just wanted to sleep, but the Son asked him to wait:
"You must learn perseverance." The Son's voice sounded stern.
"It's not enough to pull weeds, the roots and seeds must burn."

As Tim fell asleep that night, something the Son had said
Kept flashing in his dreams as it rolled around his head:
"If not pulled out—roots and all—weeds will sprout up again,
Leaving soil with far more thorns than when you first began."

The Son woke Tim up early. "There's still more weeds to tend."
The Son's instruction shocked him! "Will this job never end?
I did it for a whole day and late into the night.
It's just not fair," Tim grumbled. "No, this is just not right."

"So you don't want to serve when My work's not what you thought?"
The Son asked. "And now you want to quit the job *you* sought?
You can't give up commitment when your patience is tried.
If you want to do *My* will, *your* will must be denied."

The Son did not back off from the work He would require,
And so Tim pulled weeds all day and burned them in the fire.
And when the day had ended, and then the next day too,
Tim still pulled weeds and burned them until the job was through.

"Well done My faithful servant!" the Son said with a smile.
"You stayed the course to do My will, though it took a while.
You have had a lesson that's more vital than you know:
It's not enough to pull them, the weeds must fully go."

Then suddenly, Tim saw it—the purpose became clear.
He said, "Thanks for Your patience, and not leaving me here.
I guess I have a strong-will... but that, I'm sure You know.
I don't act as Your servant when I let my self-will grow.

"There weren't any tempters here, but I still faced these fights.
Inside me, I'm self-centered and want to have my rights.
I want to do what I want... but I want to choose Your way.
If I won't deny myself I won't choose to obey."

Though it was a lesson that came at quite a price,
The gain was more than worth it—and now the place looked nice!
But greater in importance than what was seen outside
Was the work the Son had done for Tim on the inside.

Chapter 15

After days of resting, and reading in the Book,
And talking to the Son about the journey he took;
Tim asked Him, "Am I ready to go to HereAndNow
And tell them about the Bridge You made from OneDayBow?"

The Son's eyes filled with brightness, yet sadness came through too:
"Soon you'll go and tell them all the King has done for you.
You have good news to take them of how they can be free,
But each one makes their own choice if they will come to Me.

"You've come to know the Truth here, but they haven't learned yet
That future hope's not based on *things* they can do or get.
Deep inside they're questioning what they can know is true.
The King is drawing them to Me as He once drew you.

"Now, there's one more road you'll walk before this trek is through,
To build up perseverance and endurance in you.
The road leads through the desert. It's in this barren land,
Full of fears and challenges, you'll learn how you must stand.

"The heat may seem unending, but it will purify.
You'll feel you've hit your limit, but help will be nearby.
And when this journey's finished, your faith will be like gold:
Heat can mold right character like metal in a mold."

Tim grimaced when the Son said, "You will not see My face
While trudging through the desert. But even in that place
My Nooma is still present, so choose to trust and yield.
And now one more provision: Tim, this is your faith shield.

"When winds and storms assault you and you're scorched by the sun,
Lift up high the shield in trust, recounting all I've done.
Don't doubt that I am able to help you make it through.
And when you reach the road's end, you'll clearly see that too.

"Faith in what My Word says affects the way you see—
And even in the darkness there's evidence of Me.
Look beyond the surface view, keeping My Truth in mind.
'Walk by faith and not by sight' does not mean walking blind."

But Tim had lots of questions: "Why do I have to go?
Why must I take *this* journey? Don't I already know
I can walk by faith because Your Book gives clarity?
I've had that lesson and learned it!" (But had he, really?)

The Son gave no more answers, but said, "It's time to go.
Take up the shield of faith and then walk out what you know."
Tim sighed, "Okay, I'll do it. But I still don't know why
I can't walk by the lakeside and pass the desert by."

At first the heat felt warming, and the scenery was fine.
Tim thought, *If I keep going I'll be there in no time!*
He took the shield from his hand and hung it on his belt.
He soon forgot about faith, and trusted how he felt.

But as he turned the corner, confusion filled his mind:
The desert roads were many! How could he ever find
The way that he must travel to get out of this place?
Just then a wind cloud swept the sand right into his face.

Blinded by the dust storm and cut by grains of sand,
Unable to move forward, Tim fought hard just to stand.
When finally it settled he couldn't comprehend
How vast the plain before him—a desert without end!

With sandy hands he wiped his eyes, hoping he would see
Some sign of the Son coming. Tim cried, "How can this be?
The winds are blowing harder than my strength can endure.
You said You would be with me… but now I'm not so sure."

Tim stood there for a moment, then slumped down to the ground.
Scorched by the searing-hot sand, his head began to pound.
In fear and uncertainty he wondered what he'd do.
Was it more than he'd survive? How would he make it through?

He waited—it seemed hours—expecting he would see
The Son coming to save him from that place instantly.
If this trial served some purpose, it made no sense to Tim.
Yet somehow he knew the Son could still deliver him.

Tim thought about the shield of faith. What did he believe?
Had the desert changed the Truth? The King would not deceive
Tim, or any others who put their trust in Him.
Sudden assurance whispered, *"You're not alone here, Tim."*

And as Tim started praying to know which way was best,
He saw a path more narrow but straighter than the rest.
Though weak, he set out on it and walked while he had light.
But as the darkness set in, he faced another fright.

As cold winds crossed the desert, Tim shivered in his core.
He thought he heard a tempter: *"That* King don't care no more!"
With howling in the distance, Tim's words expressed his doubt:
"Maybe I'm here forever. Maybe there's no way out."

But above his hard heartbeat, Tim sensed the faintest sound:
"Why not lift the shield of faith that you laid on the ground?
Let it be protection from what's causing pain and fear.
Act upon the Truth you know to sway the battle here."

Tim stood up and said out loud, "I'm still in OneDayBow!
I haven't left His Kingdom—His Nooma's with me now.
It was for a reason that I was given the shield;
So why does it take so long for me to trust and yield?!"

Tim took up the shield of faith and placed it over him.
Through the night he had relief from noise and frights and wind.
His heart and mind grew calm as he thought of how the Son
Had supplied the shield of faith—and *all* that He had done.

Tim wished he'd used it sooner, when the sand storms first hit.
And when the heat was blazing, he should have lifted it.
It was the shield the Son gave because He knew the place
That Tim would have to travel and the trials he'd face.

At last Tim dozed off soundly, but woke at the first light.
The journey started fresh now with lessons learned by night.
The winds of sand kept coming—the sun's intense heat too—
But when Tim lifted the shield, his faith was proven true.

Chapter 16

How long he circled those roads, Tim couldn't say for sure.
Was it days, or months, or years he struggled to endure?
He didn't like the desert and prayed he'd soon be done,
Saying, "King, I trust You, but this desert isn't fun."

And while stalled in that wasteland, uncertain what's ahead,
Tim chose to trust the Son's love and cling to all He said.
The Book became a life-line that drew him to the King.
Sometimes, to his own surprise, he'd even start to sing.

Tim endured the wilderness, but not by his own might:
His Nooma gave him power to walk by faith, not sight.
As he traveled desert roads, Tim didn't know the way,
But trusted the Son's leading throughout every day.

The desert wasn't easy—it wasn't meant to be.
It forced Tim to go further than what his eyes could see.
He learned much in the desert—but didn't want to stay.
And so he kept believing till he reached the end that day.

As Tim's path left the desert and climbed a final hill,
He heard these words inside him that brought a joyful thrill:
"All things work together for the good of those who love
The King, His Son, and Nooma—and you'll see that above!"

And then atop the hillcrest, with desert plain below,
Tim's faith turned into sight and his hope began to show.
Waiting on the hilltop was Bryce, and Brianna too,
With many others cheering, "We knew you would get through!"

They'd walked that road before him, and they had prayed him on.
As Tim saw where he'd come from, all fear and doubt were gone.
The desert winds that beat him were opening the way
To lead him on the right path—to where he stood that day.

Suddenly, it all made sense as Tim saw where he'd been,
And thought about the guidance that led him even then:
Such power, strength, and wisdom belong to the great King.
He is Lord over deserts and every single thing!

Just then Tim saw the Son's face and it was worth it all.
Though the road had been the worst the King heard every call.
By His Nooma, inside Tim, the strength he needed came
While training and reminding that battle's not a game.

"I always will be with you until the very end,"
The Son said. "Tim, you're the King's child, and you are My friend.
As it was in the desert you will not see My face,
But never doubt My Presence *is* with you in that place."

Tim asked, "Will the equipment and the Book in my hand
Continue to be with me to give me help to stand?"
The Son assured, "Of course, Tim. Before you know you'll be
In HereAndNow, equipped and prepared to live for Me.

"Each piece of the equipment that I have given you
Will be in your possession to see you bravely through.
You've learned full-well its value for standing in the fight:
Be strong in the King and in the power of His might.

"Remember, all My People are in this battle too:
The conflict is much greater than any one of you.
Encourage one another, and keep full unity,
In confidence that victory comes through trusting Me."

Confident of his future, and grateful to the Son,
Tim stood assured because of all that the King had done.
As Tim voiced his thanks, he said, "Can I ask one favor?
King's Son, please tell me Your Name." He answered, "I am Savior."

Part Three

Not Home Yet

For our present troubles are small and won't last very long. Yet they produce for us a glory that vastly outweighs them and will last forever! So we don't look at the troubles we can see now; rather, we fix our gaze on things that cannot be seen. For the things we see now will soon be gone, but the things we cannot see will last forever. (2 Corinthians 4:17-18 NLT)

Chapter 17

"Can you build a tower tall enough to pass the sky?
Can you scale that tower if you really, really try?"
"Is there something else out there beyond what we can see?
And just how do you get there? Won't someone please tell me?!"

"How many bobbles does it take for someone to win?
And if I don't have quite enough, can I try again?"
"Since I've lived a good life, and given bobbles away,
Will that help my chances when I reach my final day?"

Tim heard a thousand voices—so desperate to know—
All crying out for answers: *"Won't somebody please show*
The way that leads to freedom from fear of what may come?
Is there more to this life than a final bobble sum?"

"Listen! Can you hear them, Tim? And do you see each face?
Do you know what's on the minds of people in that place?
The bobbles occupy them, but do not satisfy
Their questions and their worries. Tim, do you know why?"

Tim couldn't see the Son's face, but he could hear Him speak:
"It's because down deep inside they know that they are weak.
They want to be in control of their own destiny,
And think that is the way to have real security."

Tim knew he must be sleeping, and yet seemed wide awake.
He heard another voice cry, *"How many will it take?*
I need to know the ending will be what I've desired.
What if bobbles aren't enough... Is something else required?!"

Again he heard the Son speak, "Tim, I'm sending you
To HereAndNow to tell them that the game is untrue.
There's no real security in any worldly thing.
Lasting hope can only come from trusting in the King.

"Tim, look beyond the vast gulf and tell me what you see."
The Son asked, "Is there beauty? Are people really free?"
Tim gazed across the chasm—a wide and sweeping view—
And saw a side of HereAndNow that, to him, was new.

After several moments passed, Tim answered thoughtfully,
"I know it must be HereAndNow, but it appears to me
Much different than I knew it when I lived in that land.
When I look at it from here I don't quite understand.

"I thought it was much bigger. And I thought we were free
To come and go as we liked. But now I clearly see
The boundaries firmly set to keep us in our space—
In permanent dependence on bobbles in that place!"

Tim spied the sole entrance at a one-way-only gate.
He then observed the town's end, at distance not too great.
A thick and solid barrier encompassed HereAndNow,
With just one real escape route: *The Bridge from OneDayBow!*

The only other exit was at the city's end:
A broad gate stood before it where shrewd tempters pretend
That passing through that portal might provide a good chance
Of winning some great future, or just some peace perchance.

But waiting their arrival was not as they had thought:
What they were receiving there was not what they had sought.
(One step past *that* exit it is clear there is no prize.
The good desired and hoped for is evil in disguise.)

Tim could see behind that gate—though through smoke, dense and gray:
Their tower up to heaven went down the other way!
And all those costly bobbles they worked for as their due
Were dumped into a heap and recycled to make new.

There was no reward there, just the sting of the lie:
"It's all about the bobbles!" is painful once you die.
Since they wouldn't love the Truth but chose the lie instead,
Their noomas don't have real life, yet are not fully dead.

"How can this be?" Tim cried out, in shock and disbelief.
"The tempters always implied that we could find relief
Beyond the city's ending—a good and prosperous fate."
Tim yelled out loud, "Don't go there! Don't enter the broad gate!"

Though shouting, none could hear him on that gate's inner side—
Separated, by their choice, from the King they'd denied.
"Those who are inside the gate have made their final choice."
Tim couldn't see, but clearly heard the Son's troubled voice.

"Oh, the harsh futility of choosing any thing
Above, beyond, apart from believing in the King!"
Deceit was there uncovered, and tempters' lies renounced,
But none could leave that sad place once their death was announced.

Tim was filled with grief over the vastness of their loss:
If only they had chosen the OneDayBow Bridge cross!
The Son paid to make the way, but each person must choose—
Before they go to their grave—to gain what they can't lose.

Tim closed his eyes in horror, then heard Savior say, "Tim,
Those alive can choose the King and cross the Bridge to Him.
People of the Book in HereAndNow can point the way.
Are you willing to do that? My friend, what do you say?"

"I know I have Your Nooma," Tim said. "But I'm concerned
That people won't believe what I tell them I have learned.
You've shown me some are fearful—but others love their stuff.
How do I convince them that bobbles aren't enough?"

The Son's voice was assuring as He said, "I promise to
Direct you by My Nooma, just as I said I'd do.
You aren't called to convince them—and some won't understand—
But never doubt your mission will go as I have planned.

"Plant the good seed of My Word, and I can make it grow:
Night and day I'll do the work, although you may not know
What's going on in someone, trust that part to Me.
In the end you'll be amazed by what you'll one day see!

"I want you to remember what I have saved you from,
But focus on things above with hope of what's to come."
Tim turned in the direction away from HereAndNow,
And looked above the landscape and beyond OneDayBow.

Tim gazed up in amazement and light covered his face
As he glimpsed the majesty of that great Final Place.
It doesn't need sun or moon—*He* outshines everything—
Nothing is more brilliant than the Presence of the King!

He will make all things new and there'll be no more dying!
He will wipe away all tears and there'll be no more crying!
Tim knew someday he'd be *Home* but didn't yet know when,
And hoped that he'd lead others to go there with him then.

What excited Tim the most? The thought that one great day
He would live there with the King and never go away.
The vision filled his thoughts as he stretched out on the ground,
And before the moment passed, his rest was once more sound.

Chapter 18

Tim had been dozing soundly, but suddenly he woke—
Had he just been dreaming or did someone yell out, "Broke!"
Tim jumped up in amazement, trying to figure how
He could be beside the Bridge he took *to* OneDayBow.

"They're broken! Hey, I told you twice not to put them there!"
Another voice was closer, but Tim could not see where—
Or who it was that yelled out… Tim was really confused.
Whoever was there shouting seemed extremely amused.

Tim slowly started brushing the dirt off of his shirt,
As a girl walked up to him and said, "Tim, are you hurt?"
"I'm not sure… I don't think so," Tim muttered quietly.
"They've stolen all your bobbles!" she shouted. "Don't you see?!"

"I really tried to stop them. I hope that they get caught!
How awful they would steal all the bobbles that you brought."
Tim recognized the girl, and then he remembered where:
She's the one he treated mean on the way to the Fair!

"My name is Makenna Linn. We've never *really* met.
You're looking kind of pale… Is there something I can get?"
Tim clearly heard her talking, but he could only stare.
He wondered what had happened—not only what, but *where?*

Tim's mind reeled with questions about *what* had occurred.
But on the ground, near the Bridge, Tim spotted the King's Word!
The Book the King had given in OneDayBow to Tim,
Was proof he wasn't dreaming—because it came from *Him*.

The belt was wrapped around him, and helmet on his head;
The breastplate over his chest, and the shoes that had led
Tim throughout his journey were securely on his feet.
The shield of faith was there too. The outfit was complete!

Tim stared at his equipment but only could say, "Wow!"
Just as the girl was saying, "…guess you don't need help now."
"Wait!" Tim interrupted, as Makenna turned to leave.
"Have you heard about the King? What do you believe?"

She stared at Tim uncertain of what to say or do,
So he continued talking, "I have good news for you!
I've crossed this Bridge to the King! You want to meet His Son?
He gave me a new Nooma!" Then she began to run!

"Hey, wait! Where are you going? You're running *from* the Bridge.
Please come back!" Tim shouted as Makenna crossed the ridge.
Somehow he had expected to have a better start.
But maybe, someday later, she'd have a change of heart.

Reluctantly, Tim left there, and as he looked around
He noticed sixteen bobbles just lying on the ground.
He said, "Did someone lose these—or were they mine before?
It really doesn't matter, I don't need them anymore.

"I wonder… do I break them or take them back to town?
Should I put them in my pack or leave them lying down?
This could be more difficult than I thought that it would—
Going back without *any* will really not be good."

Then suddenly, Tim spotted a tempter near a tree:
"Worried about lost bobbles? I'll give you some for free."
Startled by the tempter's words, Tim quickly turned and fled
Until he reached a safe spot where he sat down and read.

"Don't store up a treasure that may rust or thieves might steal.
Set your hopes on things above that are lasting and real."
Tim sighed, "I don't want bobbles—or believe tempters' lies—
I'm just afraid I'll be a freak in everybody's eyes."

Just then Tim heard some footsteps and looked around to see
Emma walking toward him, as she said, happily,
"I can tell that you've been *there*—you have His Nooma too!"
Tim cheered up and said to her, "I'm so glad to see you!"

"I met the King's Son," Tim said. "And I walked through OneDayBow!
I saw a lot of tempters, but I am so glad now
I know the King is stronger than any foe I'll meet.
By His strength I won't turn back or give up in defeat."

Tim meant each thing he'd spoken but as the words came out,
Deep inside he asked himself, *"Then what's this all about?*
Why are you so worried now? Remember you've been sent—
Not to take them bobbles but to tell them where you went.

"You don't need to be anxious if you're trusting the King.
You know He's more than able to keep you from falling."
Tim whispered a thankful prayer, "I know You'll see me through."
Then he said to Emma, "I have something to ask you.

"Does it ever bother you what people say and think?
Wondering how my friends will act makes me stomach sink!
I don't care about bobbles... but do want to fit in.
I'll look real out of place in this outfit I'm wearin'."

Emma's words were knowing as she looked Tim in the eye:
"I can't say I don't care at all, but I always try
To remember the Son says my real Home's *not* this place.
We're different from them because they haven't seen His face.

"And if we act just like them, why would they ever be
Curious to find out how the King could set us free?
As for your equipment, there's no need to be afraid.
No one else can see it's there. That's just the way it's made.

"The only thing they'll notice, besides the change in you,
Is the Book you're carrying. They need to know it's True.
You'll want to read it often, and be ready to share
With anyone who'll listen—anytime, anywhere."

Then they started toward town, before it got too late.
"Crissy is the first I'll tell..." Tim said, then shouted, "Wait!
How will I explain it, Em—why I've been gone so long?
My family must be worried that something's really wrong..."

But before Tim stopped talking, while standing in the street
His sister, Crissy, yelled out loud, "That is really sweet—
Timmy has got a girlfriend! And mom is mad at you.
It's six o'clock and you told her you'd be back by two."

"Huh?" was all that came out, as Tim looked around the place.
Emma said, "The Kingdom's not confined by time and space."
Then Tim really understood some things the King had said...
Just then Steven's basketball smacked Tim right in the head!

"C'mon Tim, leave the girlfriend and play some ball with me."
Steven jeered, while Crissy laughed. And Tim asked, "Can it be
They don't know that I'm different, or wonder where I've been?"
Emma said, "In time they will. Be patient until then."

As Emma turned the corner, and Steven threw the ball,
Tim hiked up his driveway as he heard his Mother call:
"I hope you have a reason for coming home so late."
*You're gonna be surprised, Mom—*Tim thought—*or should I wait?*

Chapter 19

Six months had come and gone since Tim crossed to OneDayBow.
He told a lot of his friends, but most of them said, "How
Can you say that you've been there and met some unseen King?
We'll believe it when we see it! Show us some *real* thing."

The Book did not impress them much. One said, "It can't be *True!*
Give us scientific proof, and carbon-dating too."
Tim answered, "Please believe me that what I said, I've done.
If you go out to the Bridge you can meet the King's Son."

But they laughed all the louder when Tim said, "Just one way
Will take you to His Kingdom, and you could never pay
For that cross with your bobbles. The Bridge exists because
The Son alone could pay the cost—that's how high it was!"

Some friends, and his family, were skeptical at best.
When Tim said, "The game's a lie!" he quickly lost the rest!
He wasn't going to give up. He knew someone must care
Enough to go and see if the Bridge is really there.

But at times Tim felt tempted to give up and go back
To just collecting bobbles and filling up his pack.
It wasn't that he believed there was any real prize,
But he got tired of being mocked and accused of lies.

The Nooma inside Tim wasn't one tempters could get,
So they didn't push the point—or even try—and yet
They heckled and provoked him and tried to prove him wrong.
Because he spoke the King's Truth, their resistance was strong.

He knew this was a battle, and knew what he must do:
Use all the King provided, and trust He'd see him through.
Knowing the Truth was vital for walking the right way,
And making good decisions throughout every day.

But the good Tim tried to do would often come out bad.
And when his patience was tried, he often would get mad.
The Book detailed instructions about how Tim should live,
But often it required more than he wanted to give.

Battling the tempters' lies was never any fun,
But the battle with his self-will was the hardest one.
He tried to choose the right way, but sometimes he did not.
And when life got difficult, he complained... a lot.

It often was a challenge to discipline his mind.
He tried to focus on Truth, but often he would find
That wrong, unruly thinking would fill his thoughts instead.
Sometimes he felt a war must be raging in his head!

Tim couldn't see the King there, but often talked to Him.
"Hello King," his prayer began, "this is Your child, Tim.
I'm sure You already know that I've made some mistakes.
I lost my temper twice today... and ate my sister's cakes.

"I'm finding out that trouble comes naturally to me,
Kind of like in OneDayBow... except more frequently.
I want to do the right thing—I want to choose what's best—
But I'm afraid I'm failing at almost every test!"

Tim knew he owed his sister a big apology.
And as for his bad temper, he'd act more patiently.
He wanted to do better, and really hoped he would,
But couldn't shake the feeling inside he was no good.

Suddenly, it came to Tim, and he remembered how
The Son reassured him on that road in OneDayBow.
It was in that very place the Son had given Tim
The helmet of salvation, and had encouraged him.

"I've rescued you from far more than you can comprehend.
I've given you a new life and count you as My friend.
This helmet of salvation deflects the tempters' lie
That says you cannot be saved, and other tricks they'll try."

Remembering the Son's words gave Tim the peace he sought,
And he was reminded that his self-will must be fought.
There were lessons still to come, and battles with deceit,
But in the King's might he'd stand and not fall in defeat.

Tim realized the lessons he learned in OneDayBow
Provided perfect training for all that he faced now.
And if he'd walk in victory, he must not forget
To keep on the equipment—*the war's not over yet.*

Chapter 20

"Dad and Mom, I'll be home late," Tim's words came nervously.
"Are you going *there* again?" Dad asked, impatiently.
His mom was much more subtle: "Now Timmy, don't you think
There's something else you should do?" Tim felt his courage sink.

His dad said, "You'll be sorry you didn't even try
To accumulate bobbles. I can't understand why
You can't be like the others. Just try to play along!"
His dad was getting frustrated: "Where did we go wrong?

"If *you* want to believe it—that talk about the King—
Though I don't agree with you... Well, I guess that's your thing.
But don't discard your future by failing to achieve
Success at gaining bobbles." Then his dad stood to leave.

Tim made himself be quiet—he didn't want to fight.
His dad was only trying to do what he thought right.
But then Tim said to his mom, "If only you would go
Across the Bridge from OneDayBow, then you two would know."

"I know that you're committed," his mom said. "That's okay.
And you're a better person in nearly every way.
I listen when you tell me the things that you have done,
But, Tim, can't you compromise? Some bobbles must be won."

His mom paused, then sharply said, "Please, try to play the game!
You've become a fanatic—*those People* are to blame.
I'm not sure you should go there, but I won't tell you 'No.'
But I would be much happier if you wouldn't go."

Tim swallowed hard and said to her, "I love you and Dad.
I never want to hurt you or try to make you mad.
But if Dad would meet the Son, it would be clear to him."
His mother's face grew softer as she reached out to Tim.

"One day I might go," she said. "But I can't promise when.
Perhaps it's best that you don't say anymore till then."
They heard some footsteps outside, and Emma yelled out, "Hey!"
"I've got to go do this, Mom," Tim said, then walked away.

He stepped out to the front yard, and Emma said, "Hi Tim.
Steven and Jess are coming." She stopped and looked at him.
"Is everything okay, Tim? You're looking really down."
The best he could answer was to nod his head and frown.

"Alli said she'd be there too. She likes to hear us sing."
Suddenly, Tim blurted out, "It is so frustrating!
How can I see it so clear, and others just can't see?
When I talk about the Bridge, why don't they believe me?"

"Timmy, can you remember," Emma spoke soft and slow,
"Before you chose to see the Bridge, did you want to go?
Until you had crossed over, did it make sense to you?
When you first heard of the King, did you believe He's True?"

Tim said, "I do remember I had my share of doubt...
But I went and crossed the Bridge so that I could find out.
I guess it wasn't easy. You're right, it took a while
To lay down all my concerns—and leave my bobble pile."

"The King is patient," Emma said. "He wants all to come
To OneDayBow and meet Him—no matter where they're from.
We're not called to convince them, but to clearly proclaim:
Real hope is found in the Truth, not in a made-up game.

"Give them time and patience, but that doesn't mean give up.
Always be respectful, and try not to be abrupt.
Remember they are watching. Believe the Son's at work.
Now we've got a job to do!" Emma said with a smirk.

As they reached the park's entrance, and side by side walked through,
Tim knew that Emma was right in what she said to do.
He would continue trusting the Son to lead each day,
So he uttered one quick prayer: "King, tell me what to say."

Chapter 21

The town had been invited to come for food and fun.
The park was getting crowded, and it was only one!
The People of the Book were there putting on a show.
Tim was asked to share the Truth with all who'd want to know.

Many were unfamiliar, but some of them he knew
Noticed he had no bobbles, and asked, "What's up with you?
You haven't been at contests, and you weren't at the Fair.
Word is spreading around town that you no longer care."

That gave Tim an opening to tell them what he'd done:
He'd crossed the Bridge to freedom—the cost paid by the Son.
They listened to his story with curiosity,
Until someone shouted out, "Nothing is ever free!

"There's got to be a catch here. Why would there be no cost
To cross a Bridge to freedom? Tim's bobbles have been lost.
Why should we believe you, Tim? You've got to show us proof."
The crowd began to break up, and people seemed aloof.

"You haven't met the King yet," Tim said, when he could speak.
"But don't be tricked by tempters to think that faith is weak.
They say we must gain bobbles or we will have no hope.
But if you ask the tempters *why*, can they tell you? *Nope!*"

"They don't want you to find out that the game is pretend,
And that you won't gain what you thought at the city's end.
If you want to know the Truth, then go out past the ridge.
You will see your only hope is found across the Bridge!"

With those words Tim stopped talking and waited for reply.
A few turned and walked away, not even waving bye.
When some appeared attentive, a woman shook her head
And strutted to where Tim stood—to dispute what he said.

"I'm glad you found the Bridge, Tim. It seems to work for *you*.
But don't try to convince me there's just *one way* that's true.
The monument is my way, and I believe it's fact.
Besides, look at these bobbles I have already packed."

She said, "I have enough to win all that I've desired,
Because to do your best will be all that is required.
Where I lay my nooma down is where my hope begins.
And when we pass the city's end, *everybody wins!"*

Many liked her confidence, and her philosophy,
Even though the things she said had no authority.
Had she come for the purpose of deceiving this crowd?
Tim thought it in his mind, but his face said it out loud.

Tim stared a few long seconds into her piercing eyes,
Wondering if she might be a tempter in disguise.
And when he held the Book up she quickly walked away,
Muttering as she passed Tim, "We'll meet another day."

A few people followed her, and others stood to leave
When Tim quickly blurted out, "You're easy to deceive!"
Tim was getting tired of not getting anywhere.
Inside he thought, *Why bother? None of them even care!*

Then Tim thought about the Book—and the belt he wore—
And prayed, "King, please do something to make them want Truth more."
It was then he thought about the peace shoes on his feet:
The good news must go forward—it's no time to retreat!

"We may not talk about it," Tim's word's came carefully,
"But deep inside we've all feared that we aren't *really* free.
We fill the void with bobbles, and desperately try
To mask our worries about the day we'll say 'Goodbye.'

"We're scared we're not good enough, and know that we've done wrong,
Even though we try to act like we are brave and strong.
The King knows what's inside us—that's why He sent His Son
To pay the price to save us, in spite of all we've done!"

"Excuse me, may I speak to you?" a quiet voice asked Tim.
Surprised, he spun around to see who'd spoken to him.
"Can I ask you a question? I have been wondering
If it's true that *anyone* can go and meet the King.

"I've had a lot of trouble and made some big mistakes.
I've got a lot of bobbles, but most of them are fakes.
I really want to go there. I need to meet this King.
But will He even let me... because of... everything?"

"Yes, *anyone* who chooses to meet the King can go,"
Tim said. "His Son is at the Bridge—He will tell you so."
Just then, Tim spotted tempters gathering all around:
They took three sacks of bobbles and rolled them on the ground!

The crowd started scattering. Everyone within sight
Was running for free bobbles—it almost caused a fight!
The tempters glared at Tim and the People of the Book,
But the park thinned out quickly as most ran off to look.

So Tim stepped up his praying, and others joined in too:
"King, please deal with the tempters and show us what to do."
A man stayed there listening. Tim wondered, *Does he care?*
He seemed to be quite wealthy, with bobbles everywhere.

"I've had all of the bobbles I'd ever care to try.
I must admit, the fact is, sometimes I wonder why
I spent my life collecting what I'll just give away,
For some uncertain outcome on that final count day."

Tim tightened the belt of Truth and spoke out fearlessly:
"The sad, certain outcome is you'll live in misery!
Once you reach the city's end with the bobbles you've got,
You'll find the reality is not what you have thought.

"I know what's past the gate, and you'd never choose to go.
If you saw what lies back there, beyond a doubt you'd know
The Great Bobble Game is fake. There's only just *one way*
To escape the tempters' lies: believe the Truth I say!"

"Who do you think that you are to say there's just *one Truth?*
I've been around a long time and you are just a youth!"
The man was now in Tim's face and poking at his chest.
Tim hoped the breastplate on him could pass this angry test!

But as the man's hand hit it, the words sprang out of Tim:
"It's not about who I am—it's all because of *Him.*
The King is the Creator, and what He says is True.
You may not believe it, but the Truth's not up to you!

"The Truth is that all fall short of what the King requires.
Each of us is far off course in actions and desires.
But while we were all wayward, and set on selfish gain,
The King knew we were helpless to make things right again.

"So He did what we could not. The King prepared the way
For us to come to Him, but there was a price to pay:
A price no one could pay except the Son of the King—
The One Who created and sustains everything!"

The man stood there silently but did not turn away.
So Tim continued speaking: "We all will bow one day,
Confessing that the Son is over all that we see.
If you bow before Him now, the Son will set you free."

Tim said, "You have been striving for some uncertain end.
No matter what you've done here, you never can defend
The reason you denied the King and refused to trust
Him to renew your nooma. If you'd have hope, you must."

The man's face started changing. He couldn't hide his tears:
"Inside my heart I'm searching. I've wondered all these years
Why I feel lost and empty. Although I've taken pride
In being rich in bobbles, I'm really poor inside."

Tim said, with deep compassion, "And that's no way to live.
What you're lacking is real hope, only the King can give.
He wants you to trust Him, and I'm here to let you know
It's not too late for changing. It's not too late to go.

"The Son is at the Bridge and will point you to the King.
He doesn't want your bobbles—He doesn't need a thing.
But you won't want to keep them. You'll see they have no worth.
Give up your hope in bobbles and He will give new birth."

Joy washed across the man's face! He said, "I'm going now
To meet the Son at the Bridge He made from OneDayBow."
And then he turned and yelled out, "Will anyone join me?
I'm going to the Bridge so the Son will set me free!"

One by one they came forward, and said, "I'm going too."
Excitedly, Tim told them, "It's the best thing you'll do!"
Inside he prayed, "Thank You, King! They're headed to Your Son!"
Tim was filled with gratitude for all the King had done.

Not everyone was happy—Tim made the tempters mad.
They yelled out behind the crowd, "You'll find that you've been had!"
But tempters couldn't stop them, no matter what they'd say,
And all who chose to take the cross met the King that day.

Chapter 22

"You said you would do it, so you need to get it done.
I know I said I'd help you, but now it's after one!"
Emma was, impatiently, attempting to help Tim.
But you couldn't miss that she was getting mad at him.

"My dad knows that I hate this!" Tim said with a sharp frown.
"He should clean up his own yard so I can go to town."
Tim was choosing laziness—and a bad attitude.
Emma had never seen him acting so mean and rude.

"You told your dad you'd do it so you could help him out.
If you meant what you told him, then what's this all about?"
Emma sounded frustrated, because she really was.
"You said you'd pay him back for all the nice things he does."

"Okay, fine!" Tim grunted out, then spun around the rake.
"I didn't think he'd say 'Yes'. This *is* my summer break!"
Tim knew he sounded selfish, but that's just how he felt.
He took his peace shoes off and then loosened the Truth belt.

"I've been here three hours, and we haven't done a thing."
Emma gathered up her stuff and said, "Tim, I'm leaving.
I hope you talk to the King about your attitude.
Next time that I see you, hope you're in a better mood."

"C'mon, Emma!" Tim yelled out, "I'm ready to start now.
My mom's roses need clipping, and I can show you how."
But Emma kept on going, not even looking back
When Tim pretended to have an allergy attack!

Tim couldn't believe she'd leave! She said that she'd help too.
Guess he had been wrong to think her word was always true.
He swung the rake wildly through a patch of dying weeds,
Then grumbled all the louder when he saw the flying seeds.

"I hate yard work—I hate it!" Tim spoke up mad and loud,
Just in time to hear thunder and see a dark black cloud.
Within a few more minutes the sky began to pour.
As Tim got wet, he snickered, "Too bad I can't do more."

Tim walked into the kitchen and told his mom, "Goodbye.
It's way too wet for yard work—I'll do it when it's dry."
"Maybe you should stay at home," his mom said, "since it's wet."
As he closed the door, Tim chimed, "Rain hasn't hurt me yet!"

Tim felt a twinge of guilt as he skated down the street—
Later he would put the peace shoes firmly on his feet.
The belt of Truth hung loosely, but it would be alright:
For now he didn't want it to cramp his style too tight.

So Tim spent the next few days doing what he wanted,
And he ignored yard work until he was confronted.
His mom said, "Tim, you promised that you would help your dad.
He's been very patient, but he's starting to get mad."

Tim already knew that, but he hoped she wouldn't say
Anything about it yet—he had plans for the day.
But then she said the one thing he wished he hadn't heard:
"Doesn't the Book say something about keeping your word?"

Tim tried to be defensive, but he knew he was wrong.
He'd been ignoring the Truth and let self-will grow strong.
He'd made his dad the promise—in fact, he had been *hired*—
Now Tim had to choose to do the work that was required.

Tim tightened up his belt as he walked out to the yard.
If he got to work right now it wouldn't be too hard.
But back in the far corner—where *the rake* threw the seeds—
A brand new crop was growing of giant, seed-filled weeds.

Tim felt sick to his stomach as his words spilled out, "No way!"
He wanted to turn and run, but knew he had to pray.
"King, I really messed this up and failed to do what's right.
But I do remember what Your Son told me that night.

"'Unless completely dealt with, more weeds are gonna grow,
And there will be more later than you can even know.'
Once again I've proved Him right by doing what is wrong.
I'm sorry I've been lazy, and chose my way so long."

Tim had lots of time to think about his selfish ways:
Pulling weeds and cleaning-up took him nearly three days.
But by the time he finished, the lesson had been learned.
Tim shouted out, "Hooray!" as the last of them was burned.

As he looked around the yard, he was glad it was done.
His dad came out and told him, "I'm so proud of you, son.
You kept your word and did it—although it took a while.
You chose to do the right thing." His dad's words made him smile.

Tim was glad he'd pleased his dad, but more than anything
He wanted him to know it was because of the King.
"Dad, I know I've been lazy and selfish in the past.
I've done the things I've wanted and put my duties last.

"The Book the King gave me clearly says that's not okay.
It tells me to respect you, show honor, and obey.
I'll be more obedient to you, and to the King."
His dad smiled and said, "Thanks Tim. The King's done a big thing!"

Tim was glad for peace shoes—that were back on his feet—
And that his dad had listened. Maybe someday he'd meet
The Son at the Bridge He made, and go to OneDayBow.
Then he'd really know that's why Tim is different now.

The day was almost over, but while he still had light
Tim needed to find Emma and tell her she was right.
His attitude had been bad, and his actions were wrong.
Emma wouldn't be surprised—she knew it all along.

Self-weeds had grown inside him. The Son said they must go,
Or there would be more later than Tim could even know.
He learned there's more to life than doing what you want to:
If you let those self-weeds grow, they might overtake you.

Chapter 23

Tim had been missing Heidi. He'd heard she moved away.
So one day he asked Emma, but she was slow to say:
"I haven't seen her lately... I'm not sure where she went.
I heard she moved someplace where bobbles are bought and spent."

"Emma, you can't mean that she..." "Tim, I don't really know
Why she felt she had to leave, or where she'd even go.
I think about her often—and pray for her—and trust
The King has His eye on her. I still believe He must."

Tim decided to find her, and so he asked around:
"Does anyone have a clue where Heidi can be found?"
No one around the nook knew, so he tried at the Fair.
There he talked to an old friend who said that he knew where.

So Tim went down to Front Street—he hadn't been before.
One person stared, then asked him, "What are you looking for?"
The one who was asking Tim brushed up against his pack,
Saying, "Why's there some book and not bobbles in your sack?!"

The kid had many bobbles, but lots of them were cracked.
He mumbled something about strangers being attacked.
The boy went on to tell Tim, "It's dangerous down here.
You should consider leaving." Tim's heart beat fast from fear.

Tim said, "I'm looking for a friend—Heidi is her name.
I haven't seen her lately... not sure she looks the same.
I'd really like to find her, and then I'm gonna leave.
I'd sure appreciate any help I could receive."

"You don't have no bobbles, so I don't have no help."
The boy laughed and walked away as Tim heard a loud yelp.
He moved in that direction to see what made the sound.
As he walked up close he saw a girl down on the ground.

Tim knelt right there beside her, and asked her, "What's your name?"
She said, "My name is Heidi." She *didn't* look the same.
Tim said, "Do you remember me?" Heidi seemed unclear.
"Heidi, you are the King's child! Why would you be down here?"

"It started out simply with one bobble and then two."
Heidi turned her face away, and sighed, "Now, I guess you
Can see they're my obsession—I'm hooked and still want more.
They don't really satisfy, but they're what I live for."

"Heidi, where's your equipment?" Tim knew she'd been deceived.
"Where'd you put the shield of faith? Think, Heidi! You've received
The knowledge of the King's love... I know you love Him too.
Put back on the helmet—He can still deliver you!"

Her voice was soft, and cracked as she wiped away a tear:
"Although I haven't asked Him, I don't think He'd come here.
I know my love for bobbles has occupied His place,
And now my greatest longing has become my disgrace."

Tim pled, "Heidi, stop that! You're going to have to fight.
You know bobbles can't help you, or make your life be right.
They cannot give you comfort. You know they hold no peace.
Cry out to the Son for help! Confess your wrongs, then cease."

Though Heidi's tears were flowing, with bobbles in her hand
She turned away from Tim, saying, "You don't understand.
I've gone too far to turn back, and I'm headed nowhere.
But thanks for your concern, Tim. I think you really care."

Tim felt his heart was breaking as Heidi walked away.
He knew he couldn't stop her, but knew that he must pray.
He wouldn't give up hoping Heidi would come to see
The power of the King's love can bring a victory.

It was several days later, by a river inlet,
Tim saw a fish swim into a skillfully placed net.
It made him think of Heidi: *Why would she choose to go?*
Why'd she leave the Truth she knew? How come she didn't grow?

Tim stood there silently as he recalled Emma's voice:
"Even though you cross the Bridge, you still retain free-choice.
Use your freedom to obey, and know that this is true:
Faith's not only what you say, it's proved by what you do.

"You must bear with the weak ones and help them to be strong.
Be willing to forgive, but be honest about wrong.
Trust the King is faithful to help them want His will.
And even if the weak fail, show them you love them still."

Tim didn't have the answers to why and what and how,
Or if he'd get the chance to tell her that even now
She can return to the King. He's willing to forgive,
But we must remember that it matters how we live.

A week later Tim returned with food and clothes for her.
The clothes came from Emma. She said if Heidi were
Willing to come back with him, she was welcome to stay.
They had a spare room at home, and it would be okay.

But when Tim tried to find her, he heard she had moved on:
Those that he asked on Front Street told him that she was gone.
He would continue praying for Heidi's safe return,
But through it came a lesson that Tim needed to learn.

The freedom we are given came at the highest price:
Treat it as a costly gift of greatest sacrifice.
Remember that the tempters would like to see you fall.
Don't settle for HereAndNow—it's not Home, after all.

Chapter 24

Every week Tim met with the People of the Book.
The King made them family, not based on how they look,
Where they live, or how they talk—their faith made them one.
Together they were stronger for the work of the Son.

Sometimes Crissy came along to listen to them sing—
Though she thought it kind of strange to sing about the King.
Three times a month on Fridays, they have a night for youth.
Everyone is welcome. They call it, "Live the Truth."

So on a Friday evening—when summer days are long—
Tim set up chairs for thirty, but prayed that he was wrong
And even more would show up. He'd have to wait and see.
Crissy offered to help him, then chattered endlessly.

"I'm glad you let me come, Tim. And thanks for asking Dad.
I can help you set up chairs, and Alli will be glad
To help us when she gets here. I think she's on her way.
She told me just this morning that she'd be here today.

"Look, someone is coming that I haven't seen before."
Crissy let go of the chair—it crashed onto the floor!
"Sorry!" Crissy yelled to Tim. "Three more are coming too."
Tim quickly prayed, "Thank you, King, for all You're gonna do."

After introductions, Emma opened with a song.
Tim's friend, Eddie, said some things—but not for very long.
Then they went to smaller groups, and Crissy sat with Tim.
"My brother's really smart," she said. "You should listen to him."

Tim took the compliment but was tired of her talk.
He thought about suggesting that she should take a walk.
Instead he broke the ice with, "Crissy's visiting too.
So no need to be nervous—she will entertain you."

With that, there was some laughter, and all were more at ease.
Crissy liked the attention and said, "I'm here to please!"
She was making jokes with them, but wanting to act dumb,
She said, "I have some questions, like, where did we come from?"

Tim sighed at Crissy's humor, and hoped it would soon pass.
One girl—Ann—was serious and said, "In science class
We talked a lot about this. My teacher knows it all.
He even did a lecture down at the shopping mall.

"We're all here by accident... by some strange, unseen force.
Twenty billion years ago, more or less, of course,
This all came from one great spark—yes, everything we see!"
Crissy asked, "A spark from where? Was it seen, visibly?

"I mean, did someone see it? Was a document found?
Twenty billion years ago... were scientists around?
I'm still not sure about *us*—that whole thing is unclear.
Not to cause an argument, but something's fishy here."

But Crissy wasn't finished—she was really thinking.
When she said the next thing, Tim felt his stomach kinking:
"And is primordial soup a valid solution
To explain origin with complete resolution?"

Ann replied, "There's science stuff that I don't understand.
I'm not sure why they'd think fish could crawl out on dry land.
Or why the monkey's uncle is still a monkey too...
It does sound ridiculous—but science says it's true."

Tim decided to jump in before this went too far:
"If you don't mind me asking, do you know that there are
Many well-known scientists who don't really agree
That evolution could be a viable theory?"

Ann then looked confused, saying "I've never heard that said.
What's in the school's science books is all I've ever read."
Tim tightened up the Truth belt, then spoke with careful tact:
"Why should unproven theory be taught as if it's fact?"

Ann replied, "It must be true if it's in science books."
But while Ann was still talking, Crissy's face made strange looks.
Then she said, "It takes a lot to trust an unseen King,
But it takes even more to believe that crazy thing!"

Everyone was laughing now, except for Ann and Tim.
Crissy caught his glimpse and said, "I'm in trouble with *him*."
Even Ann smiled then, saying, "It really is okay.
She made me think more deeply, in a different way."

Tim said, "I've learned a lot about thinking differently.
It used to be I believed what tempters said to me."
Tim tried to change the subject and point them to the King,
But Crissy interrupted, "Can I say one more thing?

"Ann, I didn't mean to laugh at what you have believed,
But if you don't ask questions you're primed to be deceived.
Not to insult your teacher—and not to insult mine—
But even *I've* read about intelligent design!

"Scientists are baffled by the cell's complexity:
Just one little cell can cause such great perplexity!
It's just my opinion, but integrity is lacked
When 'science' ignores facts and Creation is attacked."

All around the room they clapped and cheered at Crissy's speech.
Tim *never* got that response the times he got to teach!
Crissy looked uncomfortable and said, "I like to read."
Ann smiled and said, "You're smart, Criss. I think I'll take your lead."

"I never asked the questions," Ann said. "I just believed.
It makes me kind of mad to think I could be deceived.
But I got lots of bobbles from those classes that I took..."
Tim cinched up the belt of Truth and held up the King's Book.

"This is the Book I read most. This Book came from the King.
It tells how we got here—and it wasn't some spark thing.
The King is the Creator, not some strange, unseen force.
The stars, the seas, and planets have the King as their source."

Tim saw Ann was listening, but others not so much.
"You say the Book is True, but isn't it out of touch?"
One girl had some questions about relativity,
But Tim calmly spoke of its reliability.

"The Book tells of events that took place in history.
The King inspired its writing, by His authority.
Many things have been confirmed by archaeology.
It even tells of future things—that's called prophecy.

"Best of all it tells about the living, loving King,
And how His Son built the Bridge—in spite of everything.
You may not know you need Him, but believe me, you do.
If you go across the Bridge it will be clear to you."

Many listened with interest. There even was one pair
Who said they wanted to go and asked how to get there.
But one kid by the door, quipped, "How can we know that's true?
You say not to trust teachers, but why should we trust you?"

Tim hadn't made that statement. The kid wanted to squawk:
"You don't even have bobbles, just lots and lots of talk!
Why does it even matter what the Book has to say?
You know that things are changing every single day."

The kid said, "We're modern, but the Book is old and worn.
You know that it was written long before we were born.
The fact you have a copy doesn't prove anything.
What does it even matter—if there's *really* a King?"

Tim was stumped for an answer and he could only pray.
Just then Emma came over, and she knew what to say:
"It matters if His Word's right, and all *will* one day bow.
It matters if you want Truth, or lies in HereAndNow."

Then she added, "Think about all who have lived before:
They too thought they were modern... They're not here anymore.
Every generation thinks it must be best and new,
But when the lies fall apart His Word will still be True."

The kid quickly stopped talking, in fact he sat back down.
Even Tim's little sister stopped acting like a clown.
Everyone seemed serious as groups were getting done,
So Emma broke the silence: "It's time to have some fun!"

In minutes they were laughing—at games without bobbles!—
Doing three leg races and other funny hobbles.
But Crissy was still talking, and so Tim tried to hear
A conversation with a boy sitting very near.

"Criss, what do you think?" he asked. She answered, "Well, Teddy,
I believe there is a King, but I'm just not ready.
But if *you* are ready and you *really* want to know,
I think you should take your pack, count the cost, and then go!"

Tim was amazed by her words—and all she'd said tonight.
Though she hadn't met the King she did get some things right.
Then he heard her say something he hoped would soon prove true:
"Maybe if you wait awhile, Teddy, I'll go with you."

That night, Tim learned a lesson that was a brain twister:
The King can use anyone—even his own sister!
Tim knew he had been prideful and needed to confess:
Sometimes, to do the King's work, I have to become less.

As the evening ended and the last ones left the place,
Tim and Emma thanked the King for His amazing grace.
They knew that He was working and had let them be part
Of what He alone can do inside a person's heart.

And when they left the building, Tim reached for Emma's hand.
It was getting dark outside, and though he hadn't planned
To take her hand in his hand, it felt completely right.
Just then, Tim heard Criss snicker, "It's time to say good night!"

Chapter 25

On a warm spring afternoon, Tim went down on Main Street
To a sidewalk café where popular people meet.
They like to discuss ideas, and have conversations
About their philosophies, based on observations.

Tim checked his equipment: The helmet was on his head;
The belt of Truth around him; the Book he had just read;
The peace shoes were on his feet and holding to the ground;
The breastplate he wore shined as he moved the shield around.

Tim knew it was a tough crowd to tell about the King—
The latest bobble trends were much more to their liking.
A girl motioned at a chair: "C'mon, and have a seat."
Tim sat down in time to hear, "The talk's about deceit."

Tim swallowed hard, deciding to listen for a while.
A boy in glasses chimed in, "It's really not my style
To force my view on someone," he laughed, "but I would lie
If I thought I'd get ahead of every other guy."

"So lying isn't always bad, if it ends up good?"
The girl near Tim asked, laughing. "And do you think we should
Allow personal opinion to shape our morals too?"
The boy replied, "No judging! Ethics aren't up to *you*."

Then another person spoke—with long nails and short hair—
"Well, everybody does it! You won't get anywhere
Unless you promote yourself, painted in the best light.
If you're not the one who's caught, then everything's alright."

"It's all about the bobbles!" they shouted in chorus.
Then some raised glasses, cheering, "The tempters are for us!"
Tim gripped the chair so tightly he may have cracked a rung.
His heart was beating loud, but he couldn't hold his tongue.

Tim asked, "Truth doesn't matter?" A girl heckled. "What's truth?"
Then made some joke about him to the tall, tattooed youth.
"I think you're in the wrong place," the girl said, with a look.
"Maybe you should hang out with those People of the Book."

Tim felt his cheeks grow hot as their laughter hit its peak:
Mad, afraid, and embarrassed, but certain he should speak.
Inside, he prayed, "King, help me know what to say and do."
Stirred by His Nooma, Tim said, "It matters when it's you!

"When *you're* the one that's lied to, or *you've* been treated wrong;
When you find out that *you* have been deceived all along;
The standard for fair treatment tips your subjective scale.
Your truth becomes relative—but *real Truth* will prevail.

"Can you change math's absolutes? Is one plus one *not* two?
And are the months and seasons irrelevant to you?
Everyone has opinions, even if they're uncouth…
You can think what you want, but you can't disregard Truth."

They seemed to be listening—much to his own surprise—
Yet one who spoke kept staring with dark, glazed-over eyes:
"Go on, tell us what you think. The floor belongs to you."
And so Tim seized the moment to tell them *Who* is True.

"The King is entitled to decide morality:
Right and wrong's defined by *Him* with full authority.
He justly sets our standards, and this Book is His Word.
And He won't be slow to judge, no matter what you've heard.

"It may seem impossible, but HereAndNow will end.
If I stand by silently, I prove I'm not a friend.
The Book says destruction will catch many unaware.
Go to the Son at the Bridge—while you can still get there!"

The group at the table was starting to get mad.
A crowd gathered around them and things were looking bad.
Tim searched for even one face that showed concern at all.
When he did he raised the Book and made one final call.

"It matters how you live and it matters what you do,
But what matters the most is to trust the King is True.
You need His forgiveness, and I hope you won't delay
To take the Bridge the Son made—*it is the only way!*"

But when he said the last words, about *the only way,*
That's when things turned uglier. Tim heard one man say,
"Come on, let's all get this guy and throw him out of here!"
His Nooma remained strong, but Tim's body filled with fear.

Tim knew the King's Son told him that some won't understand,
But this crowd was far past that—and could get out of hand.
What was Tim supposed to do? Stay seated, pray, *or run?*
Tim knew he couldn't stop the course of what had begun.

"We're just as good as you are—you and your narrow mind!
How outrageous you'd say that there's just *one Truth* to find."
The crowd all started mocking. Tim thought they might riot,
Until a voice—much louder—forcefully yelled, "Quiet!"

Tim had seen the man before but couldn't place his name.
He calmly walked around Tim, saying, "No one's to blame.
Everybody has ideas, and everyone is free
To express their opinions based on how they each see.

"That doesn't mean that they're wrong, at least not in *their* sight.
But they can speak what they want—even if they aren't right.
In HereAndNow we can't oppose what other groups say.
All roads lead to the same place. It's a very broad way."

The man scoffed, "Some have a Book, and they insist it's true.
I've always asserted, *truth is relative to you.*
That Book about *that* King is meant figuratively:
No one with higher knowledge takes it literally!"

"That's not true!" Tim blurted out. "That nonsense is a lie!
That deception got us here and I can tell you why..."
At once the tempters jumped in before Tim could say more,
Excitedly announcing "The contest starts at four!"

In minutes many scattered, except a final few.
Tim sadly realized that it's an easy thing to do
To stay very distracted by almost anything,
Except what really matters: the Truth about the King.

The man who calmed the crowd turned and shrewdly said to Tim,
"I told you we'd meet again." Tim thought, *It can't be him!*
The man looked just like Natas, except in suit and tie.
Calm and cool, he smirked at Tim, "It seems they like the lie!"

Tim sat there, stunned and speechless, while praying to the Son:
"I don't know how it could be, but could this be the one?
The one who has used deception from the very start
Is living and active here?!" Tim felt his pounding heart.

Tim remembered *his* mud pit, and threats *he* made that day,
But also how the Son appeared and chased Natas away.
And as Tim prayed for courage, the girl he had sat near
Returned to get her knapsack and asked, "Can you come here?"

Taking Tim aside, she said, "Pretty tough crowd today!
I'm glad they didn't hurt you. I'm glad they let you stay.
And oh, my name is Maegan. I know your name is Tim.
Are you feeling okay, Tim? You're looking kind of grim."

They moved away from the man, and Tim said, "I'm okay."
Maegan said, "We should sit down. So… well then, anyway…
The Book that you have with you, I wonder, have you read
Of someone who almost crossed, but walked away instead?"

It seemed like a strange question, but Tim looked in the Book:
"I think there was a rich man once… Let me take a look.
He wanted life with the King, but wanted his stuff more.
He went away rich, but sad. What are you asking for?"

"I tried to go there two times," she said. "I passed the ridge.
The King's Son looked and saw me and waved toward the Bridge.
I came so close to crossing, but wasn't close enough
To clearly hear His welcome… and something about love.

"Tempters were there shouting, and my friends laughed at the thought
That any good could be found where bobbles can't be brought.
Accusing voices told me that I wasn't good enough,
And warned the Bridge to freedom would be narrow and tough.

"So I turned and left there, but I've always felt the loss.
All my life I've regretted I didn't take the cross.
I can't forget the Son's face. His look said He could see
All I've done, and all I am… Can He still forgive me?"

All Tim could think to say was, "He says He will forgive."
Then Maegan asked him softly, "And teach me how to live?"
Tim smiled at Maegan and said, "He can do even more.
He's able to give new life—far better than before!"

She smiled, "This time I'll do it! I'm gonna meet the King.
Will you walk part way with me? And teach me how to sing
That song about the high cost the Son was willing to pay…"
And as they started singing, the man slithered away.

Chapter 26

Another day for yard work, this time in early fall.
Tim was raking up some leaves when he heard Crissy call,
"Timmy, are you still out there? Are you almost through?
Alli wants you to play ball. Timmy, can I go too?"

Tim said, "I've got that corner to finish over there.
If it's okay with Alli, then I don't really care.
Sure Crissy, you can play too. Go get your glove and bat.
And when you get your stuff out, will you bring me my hat?"

"Sure I will!" yelled Crissy, as she ran toward the door.
"I'm really glad you're not as mean as you were before."
A lot of things had changed since Tim went to OneDayBow.
Even Crissy seemed to be a better sister now!

"Here's your glove and ball cap, Tim." Criss put them on the chair.
"Alli headed to the park and said to meet her there.
Can I look at the Book while you finish up the yard?
I really like the stories, but some lessons are hard."

"Anytime you want to, Criss, feel free to read the Book."
Tim was happy she had asked, then Crissy cried out, "Look!
It tells about the King's Son and how He made the way
So we could go to meet Him. You *really* didn't pay?"

"Nope, I told you Crissy that you cross the Bridge for free!"
Tim said to her, while smiling, "I'll take you and you'll see."
Tim waited for her answer—he really hoped she'd go.
But as she put the Book down, she firmly answered, "No.

"Timmy, I'm just not ready to make that kind of choice.
I've got lots of life to live. I haven't heard that voice
You said I'd hear inside me. I'll go there when I'm old.
But don't you worry, Timmy, my nooma won't be sold."

Though Tim was disappointed he knew he couldn't make
The choice for her. But he said, "How about if I take
You to the ridge and show you the Bridge from closer view?
Maybe, if you *tried* to know, it's something you *could* do."

But even as Tim said it he knew it wouldn't be
Enough to convince Crissy, even if she did see.
We can't believe on our own, but we chose to receive
The gift of faith the King gives—that's proved when we believe.

Crissy thought a few minutes, and then she simply said,
"I might go with you sometime—but get this through your head:
I won't be a fanatic and scare off all my friends.
A few bobbles are no big deal if they serve my ends.

"Here, let me help you finish so we can get this done.
You take life too serious and need to have some fun!
Loosen up a little, Tim. Fit in to HereAndNow.
You'll be no worldly good if your mind's on OneDayBow."

Tim knew enough to give up, but only for a while.
Crissy threw his hat to him, and Tim said, with a smile,
"I'm glad that you're my sister—although you are a pest!
Put away the tools for me, and I can get the rest."

But as she walked behind him, he thought he heard her hum
A song about the King's Son! Then she said, "You're not so dumb—
At least for a big brother, I think that you're okay.
And Tim, I will go with you to see the Bridge… someday."

"Thank You, King," Tim said out loud, "You're drawing her to You!
And I believe one day she'll go and find out You're True."
They finished up the yard work and headed to the park
As their mom yelled through the door, "You two be back by dark!"

Alli met them on the street, and told them both, "Come on!
The first inning has started and we're down by a run."
They started jogging faster while passing back the ball,
But as they started downhill, Tim took an awful fall!

Chapter 27

"Is he going to be alright? Is he going to walk?"
Tim couldn't see his dad's face but clearly heard him talk.
He heard his mother crying, and then his sister say,
"He has to walk! He's taking me to the Bridge... someday."

"Savior, am I just dreaming?" Tim prayed inside his head.
He listened for an answer, but someone else instead
Spoke: "We're doing all we can. We'll have to wait and see."
Then he slowly figured out: *They're talking about me!*

Exactly what had happened, Tim didn't really know.
The last thing he remembered was setting out to go
Down to the park to play some ball. What had happened then?
His mom's voice broke the silence: "But can't you tell us when?"

"We don't have that answer yet," another female spoke.
"It's going to take some time to determine what's broke."
And then the room was quiet. It was then that Tim found
He couldn't open his eyes or even make a sound.

He couldn't move his fingers and couldn't bend his toes.
I'm trapped inside this body and no one even knows!
"Savior, can You hear me pray? I'm in pain, and afraid!"
Tim begged, "Please, come and help me!" Then he began to fade.

Tim would wake and then he'd sleep, not knowing night or day.
All that he was certain of was there must be some way
To get the King's attention, and cause His Son to hear.
Tim was desperate to know, and overwhelmed with fear.

His mind filled up with questions he couldn't understand:
Was the fall an accident, or what the King had planned?
Why did it have to happen? Did Natas cause the fall?
In his helpless state, Tim tried to make sense of it all.

I know the King is Sovereign—He has the final say;
Because He is all knowing, He knew all things that day.
Since He is all powerful, could He have stopped the fall?
When it comes to free-will choice, is the King over all?

Tim tried hard to remember things the King's Word said,
But his thoughts and reasoning were jumbled in his head.
And both pain and confusion made it hard to pray.
With all the doubts Tim had, would the King hear anyway?

Tim longed for His appearing, or even just a word
To know the Son was with him and that He really heard
The prayers that he had spoken and knew the pain he felt.
As Tim's mind was struggling, Emma came in and knelt.

"King, I know You hear me pray, and I'm certain You care.
Tim, Your child, is very hurt. It all seems so unfair.
He tries so hard to please You. Why did this have to be?
Even now I know that You can heal him instantly.

"I'm certain that You love him—yes, even more than I.
I trust that You are working, although I don't know why
This thing has had to happen. But when will his pain end?
King, You know I hate to see this happen to my friend."

Tim couldn't speak to tell her how glad he was she came.
He didn't even have the strength to whisper her name.
Then Emma started singing a song Tim didn't know,
But as he heard the words she sang, peace began to flow.

"*My King, I am certain, nothing is too hard for You.
When we are the weakest, You have strength to see us through.
Savior, You deliver us in every fight we face,
And I believe You'll touch Tim with Your amazing grace.*

"*In Your power he can stand, and I pray he will walk.
I ask You to restore his sight, and his mouth to talk.
And when he is completely well, use Your child, I pray,
To offer others Your hope, for what they face each day.*"

Tim once again heard footsteps, then Emma's singing stopped.
Someone stood beside his bed and said, "His fever's dropped!"
His dad's voice sounded hopeful: "That's really a good sign.
I think the King has heard your prayers… and He has heard mine."

Did Tim hear that correctly? *My dad is praying too?
Savior, will You use my fall to point my dad to You?
I don't like where I am now, but I believe You will
Use my pain to bring much good. I choose to trust You, still.*

Chapter 28

Many months passed by before Tim started to get strong.
Sometimes he got impatient because it took so long.
He had hoped the Son would come and heal him instantly,
But instead he found that he must learn dependency.

Little things he'd done before seemed so much harder now.
It felt like the desert road that winds through OneDayBow.
He couldn't read the Book long—his eyes were very weak.
Even after all this time he could just barely speak.

Worst of all it seemed that Tim could not remember when
He last heard that inner voice he longed to hear again.
The Truth seemed blurred and distant, or maybe Tim could not
Make his mind recover what his memory forgot.

And when Tim felt the weakest, and when his pain was great,
He found it hard to hang on and do nothing but wait.
It was then Tim faced the foe that he dreaded the most:
Natas came—*was it a dream?*—to tempt, deceive, and boast.

"I told you we'd meet again!" Tim loathed the sound he heard!
"*That* King you thought you met that day has not kept His Word.
He said He'd never leave you, so where is *that* King now?
Perhaps it was fantasy—that trip to OneDayBow!"

"That's a lie!" Tim screamed inside. "I know I met the King!"
Tim was more sure of that fact than any other thing.
But as his mind struggled with an unseen enemy,
Accusations shot at him with full intensity.

"How do you know He is real?!" came the piercing demand.
"If He's real, why won't He come and give you strength to stand?
Where is He now while you're here? Perhaps He doesn't care.
You're sick, tired, and feel alone—that doesn't seem quite fair.

"I bet you did something wrong and now He's mad at you.
You told a lie, or broke a rule. Admit that it's true!
You haven't done what He asked—you're fickle, frail, and weak."
Tim wanted to deny it, but had no strength to speak.

"He's through with you! You failed Him! Why should He even be
Concerned with your circumstance? You know eventually
Your faith will fail in *that* King—*if* there's a King at all.
If that King really exists, would He have let you fall?"

Yes, He's real! Tim told himself, *I've seen Him and I've heard.*
His promises are all True, and I believe His Word!
His Nooma is now with me, and I know He will be
Faithful to the very end because He does love me.

Tim's strength was small and fragile, and his mind full of grief.
With broken voice he whispered, "The King can bring relief.
But help my unbelief, King, and keep me to the end.
I believe that *You will come* because You are my Friend.

"I know I've failed many times and often have done wrong.
Now I see how weak I am—I thought I was so strong!
I know that I don't deserve the kindness You have shown,
And any good inside of me comes from You alone."

Tim kept crying out in hope the Son would come to save
From all the accusations. He wished he was more brave.
But there, aware of weakness, the Word at last broke through:
"Take up the shield of faith and salvation's helmet too!"

"I'm saved by grace," Tim whispered, "through faith in what *You've* done;
Not by my might or merit, but only through Your Son.
Both Your Nooma and Your Word guarantee this is True:
You have not abandoned those who seek and trust in You."

Tim had the Book and breastplate, the Truth belt and the shoes—
And what the Son had done for him *is* still the good news.
The Truth was setting Tim free! His faith began to soar
As he lifted up the shield and *spoke out loud once more!*

"King, I know You're real because I see all that You've done:
The stars that shine; the full moon; the life-sustaining sun;
The breeze that blows; falling snow; *creation testifies!*
I'm alive and see this by the marvel of my eyes!

"Even greater evidence, beyond all that I see:
I know You are real by Your Nooma inside me.
My life changed forever when I kneeled in OneDayBow.
I will believe Your promise that You won't leave me now.

"I don't know why things happen—maybe I won't, ever—
But Your Book assures that You work *all* things together
For good to those who love You: *You are King over all!*
And You alone are able to overcome the fall.

"Your Son can deliver me, and I'm certain He will.
But if He doesn't do so now, I'll trust Him until
That day when I am with Him, there in the King's land.
But until then, equipped by Him, in Your strength I will stand!"

Darkness fled as Tim's faith rose, and the fight ended then.
That didn't mean that battles would never come again.
But Tim continued trusting, and the King made him stand,
And the struggle achieved more good than Tim could have planned!

While Tim fought that fierce battle, he didn't stand alone;
The People of the Book prayed like the fight was their own.
The King allowed the battle, but set the boundaries,
And through His mighty power brought greater victories!

Chapter 29

It had been a long time since Tim crossed at the King's Bridge.
He often thought, *Is this the day I'll see Him past the ridge?*
The time was drawing nearer, and the Book made it clear:
"King's children must be ready for the Son to appear.

"Be on guard and alert! Though you do not know the day,
The Son will come to get you and take you all away.
What has been prepared for you is beyond anything
That you can see, hear, or think—you'll live there with the King!"

Tim knew the day would come when the tempters' lies would end,
And all the greed and wrongness that no one can defend
Will be judged by the Son when He comes—*this time*—to reign.
And Tim's present afflictions would end in greater gain.

The People of the Book knew the days were getting short.
Often they were slandered by the tempters' wrong report:
"Don't listen to *those People,* and *never* read their Book.
All of those fanatics should stay inside of their nook!"

The tempters, and the mayor, had warned Tim he would face
Eviction from the city unless he would replace
The talk about "just one way", with a broader worldview.
Unless Tim changed his message, his freedom of speech was through.

But Tim would not be silenced, and would not go away.
When a crowd showed up to hear what tempters had to say,
Tim tried to turn attention away from bobble spiel,
And said—while smashing bobbles!—"The fable is not real!"

You could have heard a whisper, as everybody stopped.
One tempter was so startled, all of his bobbles dropped.
Tim had their attention now. Though shaking, he announced,
"The lie of the Great Bobble Game has to be denounced!

"The lie has lasted too long—the legend is pretend!
Those who have the most bobbles won't win at city's end.
Why would you think that bobbles have power to provide
Permanent security beyond where you reside?

"You cannot build a tower that reaches past the sky—
Or become invincible, no matter how you try.
Giving up your nooma to the tempters won't buy peace.
Only if you trust the King can pointless striving cease."

The tempters started circling the place where Tim stood,
And for about a minute he wondered if they would
Do anything to stop him—or just call the mayor.
But Tim decided to act like they weren't even there.

A person, who looked sixteen, was smiling in the crowd.
He listened to what Tim said, then waved and spoke out loud:
"I'm Joe. I've been near the Bridge and heard about the Son.
My friends packed a picnic lunch—we had some laughs and fun.

"I like some things the Book says… but not everything.
Seems narrow-minded to claim there's *one way* to a King.
But I think I'll be alright. I've heard that He loves me.
I'm better than a lot I know, and almost bobble-free."

Emma, who was there with Tim, said, "That's good, but would you
Want to know if what you think isn't completely true?"
The boy squirmed around, then said, "Well… I guess that I might,
If you don't try to tell me that what I think's not right."

(How do you answer someone who may not want the Truth?)
Tim prayed, and sensed His Nooma wanted to reach this youth:
"Faith means more than thinking that there really is *a King*.
This Book is the King's True Word." Tim held it up, smiling.

"If you don't believe it all, can you believe at all?
If we can't trust His whole Word, is He King over all?
Doubting the King's truthfulness still leads many astray
When the lie is repeated, 'Did the King really say…?'

"Denying what His Book says results in compromise,
Which leads to more deception and falling for more lies.
Trusting *some* of His Word means there's much that you're doubting.
And if you can't believe Him, why should you call Him *King*?"

Tim knew that Joe had listened, and wanted to hear more,
So he went on to answer what Joe had said before:
"You're right," Tim said, "He loves you, so much He made the way—
The *only way* to know Him—and you can meet Him today.

"The King's love is the reason that His Son built the Bridge,
And if you want the Truth you must go *beyond* the ridge.
He's willing to forgive because the Son paid the cost
For the Bridge from OneDayBow, so noomas won't be lost."

Then a girl—*Ann*—walked forward. She said, "I've heard enough
To believe there is a King, but some questions are tough.
Why doesn't he accept us as we are, here and now?
And why does He require the cross to OneDayBow?"

Tim said, "As our Creator, He gives us life and breath.
But we can't live forever—one day we all face death.
The King is pure and perfect, and in His land you learn
That living in His Kingdom is a gift you can't earn.

"Despite the wrongness in us—and we all know that's true—
The King's Son made the just way to forgive and make new.
To live past here takes something that we can't do alone:
When He revives a nooma, He restores it with His Own."

Emma said, "We have free-will. That means that all will choose
Whether to seek to know Him or doubt Him and refuse.
But we can only choose Him because He chose to pay
The price for our forgiveness—so we *can* choose His way."

Many listened intently and seemed to really care.
Tim knew the King was working and wanted him to share:
"The King is not a beggar or a sad, love-sick fool.
He doesn't need followers to validate His rule.

"He made the world we live in, and still owns it today.
It's only by His kindness that we can choose His way.
It's a fact, He loved us *first*. It's our choice to love Him."
Everyone was quiet then—till the mayor tapped Tim.

Tim wondered if he'd listened. What would the mayor say?
"This rally is illegal," he said. "You didn't pay
The fee that is required for speaking in the park.
Section Twelve restricts such use, before or after dark."

Like scattered seed, many left while Tim tried to defend
The right of free assembly. But the tempters put an end
To any hope he had of continuing that day:
When they cried out, "Free bobbles!" everyone raced away.

Tim gathered up the People of the Book who were there.
He said, "Don't be discouraged. We know this isn't fair,
But we know where we battle is the enemy's land.
Using what the King provides, together we will stand!

"The belt of Truth around us holds fast against deceit.
The good news keeps us ready, so peace shoes won't retreat.
The Book is the King's True Word, able to defeat lies.
We wear the Son's righteousness, so let's not compromise.

"The helmet of salvation reminds, renews, directs.
The shield of faith we take up links us to *Who* protects.
And prayer is our life-line of communion with the King.
The equipment from the Son can withstand anything!"

Emma said, excitedly, "We have good news to share!
Those who choose to cross the Bridge, Natas can't stop there.
So we never will give up, and we'll never forget:
We battle for a reason—that's *why* we're not Home yet."

The People of the Book stood up taller than before.
"The King gave us His Nooma, and He can do far more
Than all we can imagine!" Tim said with confidence.
United, they cheered loudly: "The King is our defense!"

And right there, beside the park, while the mayor looked on;
They all kneeled down and prayed, near the sidewalk, on the lawn.
Unashamed, they thanked the King for all that He had done
So even more can go to the Bridge made by His Son.

But what they didn't see as they knelt in HereAndNow,
Was their prayers being heard by the King of OneDayBow.
(The Son is doing far more than we can even know!)
So they lifted their requests, then trusted and let go.

132

Chapter 30

Things were changing fast now—for the bad—in HereAndNow.
Officials proposed banning the Bridge from OneDayBow
From even being mentioned—including in the nook!
The mayor tried stopping prayer and censoring the Book.

Bobble theft was increasing and counterfeiting rose,
While many made excuses for the wrong things they chose.
Folks became more skeptical of almost everything,
And made bad jokes about the Truth, the Son, and the King.

"Some will not work for bobbles, for the town's greater good."
The mayor often said that, then added, "But everyone should
Be accepting of all others, and not legislate
What we do with our own bobbles. That's what makes us great!

"But we sure won't tolerate any intolerance,
Nor excuse as different, any indifference.
If some won't work for bobbles... then they can work for ours!
And when I'm reelected we will build more towers!"

The mayor of the city was up for reelection.
The tempters all endorsed him as their first selection,
And certainly influenced all that he said and did.
A platform built on bobbles was sure to win his bid.

Harassment grew far worse as law-changing was increased.
Many made their case: "The founding fathers are deceased."
Those who'd take a stand for Truth were often forced to sit.
Sadly, some good folks grew tired of the long fight and quit.

Sometimes, Tim did get weary of standing in this fight,
But the Son said to do it in the power of His might.
This wouldn't end in failure because the King can't fail!
And in the end, all will see the King's Truth will prevail.

A doctor who was one of the People of the Book
Entered the race for mayor. She figured if it took
All of her time and money—and reputation too—
Her campaign-run might lead some to think about what's true.

Some People said she shouldn't; some People said she should;
Some People were uncertain; but she just hoped she could
Be a voice to protect life, and preserve the liberty
Of People to speak the Truth and share good news, freely.

Many listened to her plans and liked her words and stance.
But tempters had their eyes on her, looking for the chance
To ask her if her platform was based on the King's way.
Then they would twist all her words, no matter what she'd say.

Everyone grew cynical of saying what you mean.
Life's value was decreasing, and children talked obscene.
But somehow in that darkness, the Truth became more clear.
And Tim grew more determined to speak to all who'd hear.

So once again he gathered the People of the Book.
He tried to get a permit, but he was told it took
A lengthy application, and a hefty fee for use
Of the *public* park—and the mayor could still refuse.

Tim's group walked along Main Street and down to City Hall.
Tim brought along a megaphone to put out a loud call.
A crowd began to gather to listen to them speak.
Tim knew that it was no time to be silent or weak.

So there in the center of the city's government,
Tim boldly stood for the Truth and said just what he meant:
"The Son wants you to know Him, and this Book makes it clear:
Turn from your wrongs—turn to the King—His Kingdom is near!"

Just then the mayor stormed in, but he was not alone.
He confiscated Tim's Book and said he couldn't own
Something so subversive that it undermines *his* law.
But when he reached for Emma's, that was his fatal flaw!

He pulled it from her firm grip, then tripped and hit the ground.
Just then a group of People—with Books—circled around.
Their numbers kept on growing—where did they all come from?
Too many to be counted… Then they began to hum.

Tempters started scrambling as the downed-mayor shouted.
His staff rushed in to help him, but they were soon routed.
And then the People's humming turned into a loud song:
A call to stand for the Truth and not bow down to wrong.

"There's a movement in the land—People will you take a stand?
The tide has turned against the right, but the Book is still our light.
Though the conflict here is great, People we can't hesitate
To take a stand for the right, or we'll be side-lined in this fight.

"Raise your hand and say I do—Yes King, we still will follow you.
We'll speak the Truth and count the cost, so this battle won't be lost.
We're the People of the King. We'll follow Him in everything.
He will defend, and we won't bow to anything in HereAndNow."

Then everyone backed up so the mayor could step out.
"You'll be hearing from our lawyers!" was all he could shout.
Tim picked up the King's Word, and held it way up high:
"HereAndNow cannot stop this, no matter how they try.

"This place is not the real Home of People of the Book.
HereAndNow will end someday, that's why the King's Son took
On our plight and built the Bridge—*He is the Only Way!*
Despite what the mayor thinks, he too will bow one day.

"Those who haven't met the King, I hope that you won't wait:
Today you can choose His cross... tomorrow may be too late.
The King so loved the world that He gave His Only Son,
To redeem those who'll trust Him *before* this life is done.

"I'm heading to the Bridge today. This might be the last time
I'm here to point you to the Son. Be certain that I'm
Not making up some story—and you'll soon know it too.
All of the tempters' bobbles have helped to deceive you."

Alli walked forward, saying, "I want to meet the Son."
Dad, Mom, and Criss agreed: "She's not the only one."
Lora, Joe, Makenna Linn, and Jess and Steven came
To meet the Son at His Bridge. They'll never be the same!

Then past the crowds, Tim saw her: Heidi was standing there!
She waved at him, pointed up, and headed off to where
They'd meet the Son at the Bridge. Tim shouted, "Thank You, King—
Heidi has returned and many more are following!"

But others remained hardened, refusing to believe
HereAndNow could ever end, and they would not receive
The chance the tempters promised them where the city ends.
One more time, Tim yelled out loud, "Tempters are not your friends!"

Tim ached as he stood watching the ones who wouldn't go.
Their loss will be far greater than they can even know.
Tim prayed, "King, please make them go—they'd be glad if they went.
Doesn't it make much more sense that they should just be sent?

"Or, You could even show them what's past the city's gate.
I know if they saw back there they would not hesitate
To walk the path to the Bridge and take the cross today…
Yet, I know, *You alone are the Life, the Truth, the Way.*

"Even if they could see where the tower really goes,
And know beyond a doubt that the tempters are their foes,
Unless they turn to You, great King—trusting You alone—
Desires and pride will fight to keep *self* upon the throne."

And that's where many bow down to their own cunning lie:
"*It's all about the bobbles*—and maybe I won't die."
Denial of the King's Word makes no one wise or free,
Instead it digs a chasm wide as eternity.

(The need for the Son's Bridge is greater than words can say.
If you hear Him calling, don't harden your heart today.
The King Who spoke creation—by His Word it was so—
Gives free-will to all people and lets us tell Him, *No.*)

Once again Tim thought about the cost paid by the Son
To offer us His Nooma: *What more could He have done?*
One thing he was certain of, each one in HereAndNow
Has received great kindness from the King of OneDayBow.

Tim prayed with deep conviction, "King, I'm certain that You
Love everyone far more than I could ever do.
You've worked in perfect wisdom throughout eternity
To save those who trust You *now* and choose to bend their knee."

And many on that day chose to bow before the King.
Tim and Emma led them there and taught them all to sing:
"It's all about the King, now and forever, over all!"
It never really was about bobbles, after all.

Epilogue

At the Bridge, Tim kneeled down as he thanked the Son once more,
For greater love than anyone ever showed before.
Then Tim spoke these final words, I thought that you should hear.
I hope they fill your mind with peace and your heart with cheer.

"One day in the Final Place His children will be free.
Until then I pray the King will gives us faith to see
Beyond the temporary, and things that can deceive,
To His great eternal hope for all who will believe."

(No one could ever dream up a story such as this:
A King and Savior, so great, He'd die to make us His!
Everything He's done for us will be clear in that Place
Where the One Who we love now, we'll then see face to face.)

About the Author

Kathy Warden is an ordinary woman—a wife, mom, and grandma—who is the daughter of an extraordinary God! Jesus Christ became her Lord and Savior many years ago, and He is still the best thing that ever happened to her—and will be for all eternity!

Kathy has a gift for rhyming, and a passion for the Word of God. She has written Bible Studies and articles (not all in rhyme!), as well as many poems. She considers it a privilege to be able to speak and teach at women's events and retreats.

For more information on The Bridge from OneDayBow, please visit our website at www.onedaybow.com

"... Let all the world look to me for salvation! For I am God; there is no other. I have sworn by my own name; I have spoken the truth, and I will never go back on my word: Every knee will bend to me, and every tongue will declare allegiance to me." (Isaiah 45:22-23 NLT)

You must have the same attitude that Christ Jesus had. Though he was God, he did not think of equality with God as something to cling to. Instead, he gave up his divine privileges; he took the humble position of a slave and was born as a human being. When he appeared in human form, he humbled himself in obedience to God and died a criminal's death on a cross. Therefore, God elevated him to the place of highest honor and gave him the name above all other names, that at the name of Jesus every knee should bow, in heaven and on earth and under the earth, and every tongue declare that Jesus Christ is Lord, to the glory of God the Father. (Philippians 2:5-11 NLT)